A DANGEROUS PROMISE

Nellie led the Texas cowboy's sorrel to the pool, giving Slocum a sideways look. "I sure hope you ain't as mean as Shorty said you was, Mr. Slocum. I've had enough bad treatment to last me the rest of my life, an' I'm sure not lookin' forward to tellin' Bill about why I was gone from Abilene for so awful long."

"Will he take off after those men?" Slocum wondered out loud.

Nellie's gaze fell. "Not likely. He'll blame it on me for workin' the cribs when he told me not to. He's liable to slap me around some."

Slocum turned to her. "I promise I won't let that happen, Nellie."

She couldn't look at him. "You don't know Wild Bill too good or you wouldn't be sayin' that."

DON'T MISS THESE
ALL-ACTION WESTERN SERIES
FROM THE BERKLEY PUBLISHING GROUP

THE GUNSMITH by J. R. Roberts
Clint Adams was a legend among lawmen, outlaws, and ladies.
They called him . . . the Gunsmith.

LONGARM by Tabor Evans
The popular long-running series about U.S. Deputy Marshal
Long—his life, his loves, his fight for justice.

SLOCUM by Jake Logan
Today's longest-running action Western. John Slocum rides
a deadly trail of hot blood and cold steel.

BUSHWHACKERS by B. J. Lanagan
An action-packed series by the creators of Longarm! The
rousing adventures of the most brutal gang of cutthroats ever
assembled—Quantrill's Raiders.

DIAMONDBACK by Guy Brewer
Dex Yancey is Diamondback, a southern gentleman turned
con man when his brother cheats him out of the family for-
tune. Ladies love him. Gamblers hate him. But nobody pulls
one over on Dex . . .

WILDGUN by Jack Hanson
Will Barlow's continuing search for his daughter, kidnapped
by the Blackfeet Indians who slaughtered the rest of his family.

JAKE LOGAN

SLOCUM AND WILD BILL'S WOMAN

JOVE BOOKS, NEW YORK

This is a work of fiction. Names, characters, places, and incidents are
either the product of the author's imagination or are used fictitiously,
and any resemblance to actual persons, living or dead, business
establishments, events, or locales is entirely coincidental.

SLOCUM AND WILD BILL'S WOMAN

A Jove Book / published by arrangement with
the author

PRINTING HISTORY
Jove edition / September 2000

All rights reserved.
Copyright © 2000 by Penguin Putnam Inc.
This book may not be reproduced in whole or in part,
by mimeograph or any other means, without permission.
For information address: The Berkley Publishing Group,
a division of Penguin Putnam Inc.,
375 Hudson Street, New York, New York 10014.

The Penguin Putnam Inc. World Wide Web site address is
http://www.penguinputnam.com

ISBN: 0-515-12909-7

A JOVE BOOK®
Jove Books are published by The Berkley Publishing Group,
a division of Penguin Putnam Inc.,
375 Hudson Street, New York, New York 10014.
JOVE and the "J" design
are trademarks belonging to Penguin Putnam Inc.

PRINTED IN THE UNITED STATES OF AMERICA

10 9 8 7 6 5 4 3 2 1

1

John Slocum was down on his luck. His horse had thrown a shoe, exposing the soft inner part of its right forefoot to every sharp stone on the trail between Newton and Abilene. And there was plenty of razorlike flint in this part of Kansas Territory to bring a good horse up lame. They were called the Flint Hills for good reason. Scant grass grew in clumps across the prairie where tens of thousands of longhorn cattle were driven to the railheads from Texas along the Chisholm Trail. Flint chips in the thin soil crippled cattle, horses, and men in this brutal country. Water was as scarce as grass during the summer in this section of Kansas and a man had to be prepared for it. Finding a water hole or a creek with a seep spring hidden below sand in a dry streambed could mean the difference between life and death, and a traveler had to know where to dig.

He'd made the acquaintance of a traveling drummer down in the Nations, finding his company a welcome relief from the quiet while riding alone. Barnaby Watson rode a mule, a beast better suited for dry, rough country, although Barnaby was less able to tolerate the late summer heat than his animals. He led another mule loaded with packs; packs containing the latest offering in mother-of-pearl buttons and fasteners being marketed by his employer in St. Louis. He preferred to be called a company representative.

Barnaby wore attire ill-suited for the heat—a dusty-brown suitcoat and trousers, lace-up shoes, and a bowler hat coated by chalky alkali dust. He frequently mopped his face with a soiled handkerchief. Barnaby was in his forties, slightly overfed, with a strong inclination toward distilled spirits. At the present, he was without so much as a drop of whiskey, a complaint he voiced all too frequently while they rode north.

"I can't remember when I've been so hot, or so thirsty," Barnaby said, wiping his neck and cheeks, his cardboard shirt collar loosened so his string necktie hung low across his ample belly. "I daresay I'd offer a man as much as ten dollars in hard coin for a pint bottle of whiskey. Even rotgut flavored with tobacco would fetch my highest price."

"Whiskey only makes a man thirstier," Slocum said, paying close attention to his bay gelding's limp. "Water is what you need."

"Water can't make a man forget this god-awful place. Why the hell would anyone live in Kansas?"

Slocum only meant to humor him. "Drovers who've come up this trail from Texas claim there's three kinds of suns in Kansas Territory, the sun burning down on us now, sunflowers, and sons of bitches. It takes a man with a hardheaded streak to settle here, I'll agree on that."

"I suppose it's the new cow towns, all the painted whores and gambling parlors," Barnaby said. "There's a new one springing up somewhere in Kansas every year. I hear Dodge City is growing like a weed, which means my company will only give me a larger territory to cover with my buttons and fasteners. I can barely cover the territory they've given me as it is. Dodge is a hundred miles or more to the west of us, at old Fort Dodge. I hear it's a boomtown."

"I suppose every whore needs buttons or fasteners once in a while," Slocum replied, gazing at the horizon now. "We shouldn't be too far from Abilene. Maybe half a day's ride, if my horse don't go plumb lame before then."

"I don't trust horses," Barnaby said. "They have a tendency to run off when you least expect it. A mule, on the other hand, can scarcely be made to run at all. I may be slower arriving at my destination aboard a mule, but I know I won't be carried off into the brush by some cold-jawed steed who refuses to listen to the bridle bit."

"To each his own," Slocum said. "A mule kicks harder'n an eight-pound sledgehammer and there's some creeks a mule just won't cross. I never was all that inclined to have a creek keep me from my destination. A man could die of old age waiting for a mule to make up its mind to cross shallow water."

"A mule's disposition requires understanding," Barnaby explained. "They are quite intelligent creatures, in fact. I shall always select a mule over a horse. When a traveling man needs dependable transportation, a mule makes the most sense for someone who's seldom in a hurry."

"Just so's there ain't any water between you and where you aim to go."

"Let's not talk about water right now," Barnably said, as he wiped his forehead again with his handkerchief. "A cold glass of water in this insufferable heat would be a treasure . . . worth its weight in gold."

"I thought you said you wanted whiskey?" Slocum

asked, a wry grin twisting the corners of his mouth.

"Anything wet sounds delightful. The last two water holes we came across were bone dry. I pray we won't die of thirst here in Kansas. This would be a terrible place to perish."

"It's August, Mr. Watson . . . August in Kansas, just about the worst combination there is. There'll be water at Willow Creek, a good five or six miles ahead. We may have to dig in the sand for it. One thing to remember in dry country . . . find the tallest and greenest cottonwood tree next to a dry streambed. Dig a hole in the sand. You'll strike water sooner or later. It's a lesson I learned from an Apache scout years ago."

Barnaby gave him a surprised look. "You make the acquaintance of redskinned savages, Mr. Slocum? From what I've been told about them, you are lucky to be alive."

"Not all of 'em are warlike. Some got tamed down by the army and now they're peaceful enough. Worst bunch I ever ran across is Comanches. Never met one who was agreeable when it came to white men."

"The ones I saw in the Nations were a pitiful lot," Barnaby remembered. "They were filthy . . . a pack of beggars, and they had a terrible smell."

Slocum knew Barnaby was talking about the Osage tribe, a sad reminder of what defeat at the hands of the U.S. Cavalry could do to a once proud tribe. "Some of it ain't their fault," he said, casting a glance along an empty horizon before them. "The army has got 'em starved down to nothing. Took away their horses and the buffalo. Didn't leave 'em much from their old way of life. They ain't got much dignity left, or much of anything else."

"But they scalped innocent white people, Mr. Slocum. It seems they're getting what they deserve."

"There were a few bad ones. Trouble is, all the rest have had to pay for what a few renegades did."

"I had no idea you were an Indian sympathizer."

"Wouldn't make no difference what color they were. Sad to see men and women of any race go hungry."

Barnably pulled off his derby to sleeve sweat from his forehead. "Going thirsty is worse, if you ask me. I'd up my price for a pint of whiskey to twelve dollars right now."

"Ain't many whiskey peddlers out here, Mr. Watson, so I reckon you can save your money. I never tasted a bottle of whiskey worth twelve dollars."

"I'm in desperate need. My throat has never been so dry and my canteen has been empty since yesterday. Whiskey or water, I'd pay for either one."

"Too bad a man can't drink money," Slocum said. "In this part of Kansas, money don't amount to much besides added weight your mule has to carry."

Now Barnaby gave him a worried glance. "You wouldn't be planning to rob me, would you, Mr. Slocum? I had judged you to be an honest man . . . however I must warn you, I carry a pistol under my coat."

Slocum chuckled. "If I'd meant to rob you I'd have done it a long time ago, and that little .32 Smith & Wesson you've got ain't big enough to stop me."

"I notice . . . you carry a great many guns," Barnaby said, as though he might still be doubtful.

"I wear a Colt .44 around my waist. The rifle is a Winchester 'Yellow Boy' of the same caliber. That little shotgun tied to the pommel of my saddle is a Greener ten-gauge, sawed off so it makes a mighty wide pattern."

"But why so many guns? You said you were in the blooded racehorse business up in Denver."

"Horses—good race stock—is the way I make my

living, but there are times when I take a job for a railroad or a bank, if they've got troubles."

"Troubles?"

"Troubles with robbers and holdup men. Sometimes I get asked to bring back money robbed from a bank or a train."

"Then you're a bounty hunter?"

"I've never liked that handle. Detective sounds fancier to me."

"But you've killed men in . . . this line of work."

"A few. Can't say as any of 'em didn't deserve to die. I make it a practice to ask a gent to come quietly when I catch up to him. If he refuses, then my hand is forced."

"I've never met an honest-to-goodness bounty hunter, Mr. Slocum."

"I told you I didn't care much for that handle."

"Sorry. You're a detective. A private investigator for the banks and railroad companies."

"Sounds better, don't it?" Slocum asked, leaning out of the saddle to examine his bay's front hoof, when the animal's limp became more pronounced. "Soon as we get to Willow Creek I'm gonna have to fashion a hoof pad out of a piece of leather. My horse ain't gonna carry me much longer with a bad leg."

"How can you make a horseshoe out of leather?" Barnaby wanted to know.

"The way some Indian tribes did in rough country. You make a boot out of leather and saddle strings. I'll have to cut off part of my saddle skirt to make it, but it's a helluva lot better than walking the rest of the way to Abilene. This bay's gonna need a few days of rest, after I find a good blacksmith."

"Abilene can be a dangerous place . . . full of gunmen and cardsharps and the like. Then there's Marshal Wild Bill Hickok to deal with. When he's drunk, which is fairly often I'm told, he can be as rowdy as a drunken cowboy. He killed one of his own deputies last year. He insisted it was an accident, but most folks who know Hickok swear he was drunk at the time."

"I've never met Hickok," Slocum said. "I've heard a lot about him."

"He's quite a character. His hair is longer than a woman's and he dresses in buckskins most of the time. He wears a pair of pistols with the butts turned backward. Most everyone is town is afraid of him."

Slocum wondered if Hickok could be as dangerous as his reputation. Accounts of his exploits sometimes differed. It was an eastern writer who gave him his name, Wild Bill. "I'll try to make his acquaintance while I'm there," he said.

"Be very careful around him when he's drunk, Mr. Slocum. I have it on good authority he's most unpredictable."

"I'm always real careful, Barnaby. It's one reason I'm still alive. There's a helluva lot of truth to the old saying that a man can't be too careful."

They crested a low hill. Off in the distance, Slocum could see a dark green line of cottonwood trees. "Yonder's Willow Creek, Mr. Watson. Won't be long till we're diggin' in the sand for water, unless we get lucky enough to find a pool someplace where the creek makes a bend."

"Water," Barnaby whispered. "My tongue was beginning to feel like it was swollen."

"Like I said, this is August in the Flints. One reason none of the big cattle herds come this way so late in the year. We've been passing piles of bleached cow bones for two days, in case you ain't noticed."

"I noticed," Barnaby replied, licking his cracked lips. "I was beginning to think our bones would join them."

Slocum stood in his stirrups for a better look at the creek. He saw saddled horses tied in the shade of the cottonwoods. "It looks like we'll have company," he said.

As a precaution, out of old habit, he loosened the hammer thong on his .44.

2

Five horses were hobbled on short grass below the cottonwoods as Slocum and Barnaby approached Willow Creek. Four men and a slender blonde girl watched them ride up. A bearded cowboy wearing a pistol and leather chaps left the bank of the stream to give Slocum and the drummer a closer inspection. There was no friendliness on the face of the hard-bitten cowhand who stood between them and a pool of water where the creek made a turn beneath the trees.

"Howdy, gents," the cowboy said, his right hand dangling near his gun. "This spot's taken. Find yourself another place to rest an' water them nags."

Slocum paid him short notice, watching the other men briefly before he reined his limping bay to a halt. "Howdy," he replied in kind. "Just passing through. Need water for our animals, if it ain't too thick with alkali. But we don't have time to look for another watering hole."

"Never can be too careful 'bout strangers," the drover said, a suspicious knot wrinkling his forehead. "Seems

9

you boys look peaceful enough. Climb down an' water your stock, but be quick about it."

It was then Slocum noticed the girl had her wrists bound together with rawhide. "What did the little lady do to deserve being tied up?" he asked, remaining aboard his gelding. "You boys got some sort of legal authority to tie her up the way she is?"

"Ain't none of your affair, stranger. If you're the nosey type, then keep on ridin'."

Slocum quickly figured the odds. Four men, all wearing iron, were watching him. None of them had badges pinned to their chests. Two cowboys standing next to the creek wore gun belts buckled high around their waists, marking them as ordinary trail hands. But the bearded gent who stood before him had his Colt holstered on his leg, tied down. And a fourth cowboy was leaning against the trunk of a tree off to the left, his cold gaze fixed on Slocum. A notched gunslinger's holster rode low on his thigh, held in place by a thin strip of rawhide.

"You don't sound all that neighborly," Slocum said, his voice even, toneless.

"We ain't neighbors, mister," the black-bearded gent said as his fingers curled near the butt of his pistol. "We came to this water hole first. By right of possession, it's ours to do with as we please."

Slocum let the remark pass for the moment. "What did the woman do to deserve having her hands tied up?" he asked again, as his own gun hand moved inches closer to his .44-.40. She was pretty, in an unwashed way. She wore a tattered dress, and there were bruises on her cheeks and neck.

"I done told you it ain't none of your goddamn business, stranger. Best you keep on ridin'. You just wore out your welcome here."

"My companion and I are thirsty," Slocum said. "And my horse, along with his mules, need water. This looks like the only pothole in Willow Creek for half a mile in either direction, so I figure we'll just get what water we need here. No sense in riding our mounts any farther than we have to in this terrible heat."

"Maybe you wasn't listenin'." The cowboy said it hard, with meaning behing it.

Slocum's irritation had reached its limits. In a single, practiced move, he swept his Colt from its holster, thumbed back the hammer, and aimed it down at the bearded cowhand. "I was listening real close. Not a damn thing wrong with my ears. The problem was, I didn't like what I was hearing. Made me think you boys might want to swap lead over a pool of water . . . seems a shame to waste good gunpowder over something like that. Hell, it ain't nothing but water."

The cowboy tensed, staring into the barrel of Slocum's revolver. Slocum had him cold, but his attention was on the other three men to see if they were ready to make their play for a gun. He could drop any one of them, perhaps all three, before the dim-witted cowhand in front of him could claw his gun from leather.

It was the silent one partially hidden in the cottonwood's shade that held his attention.

He turned his gaze back to the bearded gent when no one made a move toward a weapon. He heard Barnaby Watson draw in a quick breath.

"Like I said, asshole, I didn't like what I was hearing about me and my traveling companion having to ride past this pool, so we're gonna fill our canteens and water our animals anyway." Slocum said it with his teeth clenched, the muzzle of his gun aimed at the cowboy's skull.

The cowboy jutted his jaw. "There's four of us, in case you can't count."

"I can count real good. I ain't altogether sure I can kill the four of you before any of you fire a shot, but you can be damn sure of one thing—"

"What's that?" the drover demanded, the muscles in his gun hand stiff, tensed.

"You're gonna be the first son of a bitch to die. If any one of you goes for a gun, I'm gonna put a tunnel plumb through your empty head. This is a Colt .44-.40. That means forty grains of gunpowder will be pushing my slug through you goddamn skullbone. In case you ain't never seen one, a .44-.40 bullet makes a helluva hole."

"That'd be murder, if I don't reach for my gun," the man said, his tone somewhat softer now.

Slocum smiled a humorless smile. "Won't be no witnesses, 'cept for my friend on the mule, and he'll swear to my side of the story, that your reached for your gun first. Won't be anybody left alive to claim otherwise, 'cept for the woman, and I don't figure she'll say any different since she's got her hands tied together. I judge she's here against her will anyhow, if I can tell by them bruises on her face, so it's my guess she'll swear to damn near anything I ask her to."

From the corner of his eye, he noticed that Barnaby had drawn his .32.

"I can shoot one of them, Mr. Slocum," Barnaby said, although his voice lacked real conviction.

One of the drovers beside the creek spoke up. "Are you John Slocum?" he asked. "I heard the drummer call you Mr. Slocum an' that's a downright unusual name."

"Not that it's any of your business who I am," Slocum replied, "but you've got my name right. I'm John Slocum, if what you want is an introduction."

The drover spoke again, addressing the bearded cowboy. "If I was you, Deke, I wouldn't pull no gun just now. I know this feller . . . by reputation. You damn sure don't wanna mess with John Slocum or we'll be diggin' you a grave. This flint ground is hard as hell an' we ain't got no shovel. Besides, it's way too hot to be diggin' a six-foot hole."

"Who the hell is John Slocum?" the man named Deke asked over his shoulder.

"Bounty hunter. A killer. If you aim to live long enough to see another sunrise, I'd apologize to Mr. Slocum an' let him an' his partner have all the water in the whole damn creek, if he wants it."

"How come you know 'bout him?"

"How come you don't? He's killed more men than there is ticks on a hound dog. If I was you I'd be real polite an' keep my mouth shut."

Deke's muscles relaxed and his face paled a little. "I reckon I was out of line, Mr. Slocum," he said. "Help yourself to the water. You won't get no more trouble from us. We was fixin' to leave anyhow."

"Have you actually killed *that* many men, Mr. Slocum?" Barnaby asked as he put his pistol inside his coat.

Slocum ignored him for the moment. He spoke to Deke. "Why are the woman's wrists tied?" He kept his gun aimed down at the cowboy's face.

"She robbed Shorty of all his drover's pay."

"That's right," one of the cowboys near the creek added, pointing to the blonde girl. "She ain't nothin' but a damn crib whore noways. When I took my britches off, she emptied out my pockets an' stole every dime I had . . . three months' pay fer comin' up from Matamoros with a herd of longhorns."

"It ain't so!" the girl exclaimed. "I never robbed him. He smelled so damn bad I wouldn't buck-jump him 'less he took a bath. It made him mad, so he slapped me down an' tied me up to take me with 'em back to Texas. I never smelled a skunk that was any worse stinkin' than him!"

"That's a goddamn black lie!" Shorty bellowed, taking a step toward the girl.

"Stay right where you are," Slocum demanded. "I'd hate like hell to put a hole in a man because he didn't have regular habits with bathwater and soap."

"She's a lyin' bitch!" Shorty protested. "I took a bath the week before we got to Abilene."

"It damn sure didn't smell like it!" the girl shouted, her face turning red.

"Untie her hands," Slocum said, wagging the barrel of his gun in Shorty's direction. "Do it real slow, and make sure you keep clear of that pistol you're wearing."

"You mean you're gonna let the bitch go?" Deke said, some of the anger returning to his voice.

Slocum shrugged. "If you boys believed this woman robbed your friend, you should have filed charges with the city marshal or the county sheriff. My eyes are pretty damn good and I don't see any badges on none of you."

"Shit," Shorty muttered, sauntering over to the girl to untie her hands. "She's a goddamn thief an' I've lost me three months' wages."

"Ride back to Abilene and file your charges," Slocum said again. "Otherwise, keep your mouth shut and take that strip of rawhide off her wrists."

Shorty did as he was told, glowering at the woman while he was about it.

"Are you truly a manhunter?" Barnaby asked for the second time, almost a whisper. "You told me you were a railroad detective, and that you were in the race horse business. Have you actually killed a lot of men for money?"

"I don't keep a count," Slocum said, as soon as the

girl's arms were free. He spoke to the woman now. "Get aboard one of those horses, little lady. You're riding back to Abilene with us."

She rubbed red places on her wrists and nodded once, moving over to a sorrel gelding.

"That horse belongs to us," Deke said. "We brung it up with us from Texas."

"You can present your proof of ownership at the marshal's office," Slocum replied. "Meantime, the woman is riding it back to Abilene, which is where you took her against her will. If you can prove the gelding is yours, I'm sure the marshal will release it to you."

"That's horse theft," Deke snarled, bunching his heavy shoulders. "You ain't gonna get away with this. I don't give a damn who you are."

"Take it up with the city marshal," Slocum told him. "Now you boys climb on your horses and clear out of here before I change my mind."

"Change your mind about what?" the lanky cowboy under the tree said quietly.

Slocum turned to him. "About a couple of things."

"You gonna tell me what they are, mister?"

"No reason not to. First thing I'd aimed to do was kill all four of you. I decided against it. For now. Second thing was, I'd figured to haul you back to Abilene to face legal charges for abducting this woman. I'd imagine it would fetch you at least thirty days in jail."

"What makes you so damn sure you could get either one of 'em done?" the gunman asked, pushing away from the tree like he meant to brace Slocum. He let his gun hand fall to his side, near his pistol.

"Experience," Slocum told him calmly.

"Experience? Experience with what?"

"Facing yellow bastards like you," Slocum said. "If you had any balls, you'd have gone for that gun when you had the chance. But you didn't. And I'll tell you why. You ran short of nerve. If you thought you could take me, even with all your friends here to back you up, you'd have tried it." He let a moment pass while he stared into the man's eyes. "But you didn't. It's because you're yellow. You never face a man unless you're sure you've got the advantage. Even with three guns behind you, you didn't go for your pistol. Because you're a goddamn coward, and if you or your partners have any doubts, I'll swing down off this horse and holster my gun so we can test each other. The call is up to you, stranger."

"You talk mighty big, Slocum," the cowboy said.

"That's because I can back it up. Now take that pistol out of your holster and drop it on the ground. Same goes for the rest of you. Then climb aboard your goddamn horses and hightail it out of here, before I change my mind and kill every last one of you. I'm tired of all this loose talk, and I'm mighty damn thirsty."

3

"Thank God we got out of this difficulty without any trouble," Barnaby said, as the four cowboys rode off toward the south, looking back over their shoulders to make sure no lead was following them toward Texas. "I feared we would be involved in something serious."

Slocum walked over to the girl, paying no attention to Barnaby's concerns. "Time we introduced ourselves," he said. "I'm John Slocum."

"I'm Nellie. Nellie Cass, an' I'm so grateful for what you done for me."

Barnaby got down off his mule to stand beside Slocum, his handkerchief moving across his brow. "I am Barnaby Watson of the Saint Louis Fastener Company," he said, his cheeks flushed from the heat, and from being so close to the girl. "Those men were treating you roughly. I'm glad Mr. Slocum and I happened to come along when we did."

Nellie was staring up at Slocum. "I didn't rob nobody like they said I did," she whimpered. "It was all a lie. That short cowboy had the worst stink I ever smelled in

17

my whole life, but I didn't take none of his money. I swear I'm tellin' you the truth."

Slocum grinned. Nellie was prettier than he first imagined, and quite a bit younger, perhaps twenty or so. She had straight blonde hair hanging below her shoulders, deep green eyes, and a smooth oval face with high cheekbones. Her dress, what was left of it after her captors ripped it in several places, was a pale yellow, faded by too many washings. "No need to explain it to me, Nellie," he said. "You don't owe us any kind of explanation."

"None whatsoever," Barnaby added, his eyes on the woman's ripe breasts and twisted nipples, jutting through thin cotton fabric that was torn in front where a few buttons did a poor job of closing it. "Those men were nothing but common ruffians and I didn't believe a word they said about you. You don't look like a thief to me."

"I'll have to explain it to Bill," she said, averting her gaze from Slocum.

"Who's Bill?" he asked, wondering why it made any difference to her.

"Bill Hickok," she said.

"The City Marshal of Abilene?" Slocum asked, after hearing so much about the lawman.

"Yeah. He's gonna be mad as hell . . . if you'll excuse my bad language."

"Why is that?"

"He didn't want me to work the . . . cribs no more, on account of he said I was his woman. I told him he didn't own me like I was a horse, or somethin'."

"I take it you do work the cribs from time to time," Slocum said.

She needed time to phrase her reply. "When I need money. Bill don't give me no money, 'cept when he's real drunk. But please don't tell him I said that or he'll be mad at me worse'n ever."

"No need to worry, Nellie. All Mr. Watson and I intend to do is see you safely to Abilene. What happens from there on is up to you."

"I'm real obliged. Those men . . . they held me down last night an' . . . I reckon there ain't no nice way to say it . . . they had their way with me."

"Is that how you got the bruises on your face and neck?" he wondered. "Appears they were a mite rough on you, and your dress is torn."

"Yeah. The big one with the dark beard . . . he hit me a whole bunch of times." Tears formed in her emerald eyes. "He pulled my dress off an' throwed me down next to the creek. You was lucky, Mr. Slocum."

"How's that?"

"The other feller . . . the man standin' over yonder under that tree . . . he's a gunslick by trade. Bill told me to stay wide of him, that he was a real bad man."

"What's his name?"

"Cole. Bob Cole. He ain't nothin' but a killer, accordin' to Bill."

Slocum laughed out loud. "If he was such a mean hombre, I can't figure why he didn't make his play. I gave him the chance to prove himself before they rode out of here. He didn't show me much."

"Is it true about you?" Nellie asked, "What Shorty said 'bout you bein' a bounty hunter?"

He chose his answer carefully. "I've brought in a few men wanted by the law for various crimes. Not all that many, if you want a tally. It's not the sort of thing I keep accounts on, if you know what I mean."

"Was they dead?" she persisted, taking a half step back from him.

"Some. Not all of 'em. The ones who figured they

were faster with a gun came tied across their saddles. I gave 'em a choice . . . to come quiet, or to test their luck at the draw with me."

Nellie blinked. "Then I reckon Bill would say you're a bad man, too."

"I don't know Marshal Hickok. And I doubt if he knows about me."

Barnaby spoke up. "That one fellow who went by the name of Shorty knew who you were, Mr. Slocum. He warned the others not to pull a gun on you."

"A reputation's a funny thing," Slocum explained, turning to his bay to loosen its saddle cinch before he led it down to the water. "Some men don't deserve the mean reputations they've got, and some gents are a hell-uva lot meaner'n folks think they are. It depends on who's doing the talking, I reckon."

Barnaby led his mules toward the creek bank, shaking his head as he went. "Those four cowhands sure paid attention to your reputation, Mr. Slocum. They talked tough, until Shorty said his mind in regards to you. They became quite peaceful afterwards."

Slocum led his bay down for a drink at the edge of a muddy pool. "All that really matters is no blood was spilled. If a few words got that done, it suits the hell out of me. I'd much rather talk than shoot . . . when I'm given a selection in the matter."

Nellie led the Texas cowboy's sorrel to the pool, giving Slocum a sideways look. "I sure hope you ain't as mean as Shorty said you was, Mr. Slocum. I've had enough bad treatment to last me the rest of my life, an' I'm sure not lookin' forward to tellin' Bill about why I was gone from Abilene for so awful long."

"Will he take off after those men?" Slocum wondered out loud.

Nellie's gaze fell. "Not likely. He'll blame it on me

for workin' the cribs when he told me not to. He's liable to slap me around some."

Slocum turned to her. "I promise I won't let that happen, Nellie."

She couldn't look at him. "You don't know Wild Bill too good or you wouldn't be sayin' that."

He let her remark pass, promising himself he'd see to it that no harm came to Nellie after they reached Abilene.

He set about to fashion a hoof pad for the sore-footed bay out of saddle skirt leather, working slowly, carefully, with his Bowie knife while Barnaby and the girl looked on. Every now and then he glanced up at Nellie, only to find her staring at him with a hint of a smile on her face.

Later, as Slocum was fitting the pad to the horse's hoof, Nellie walked down to the water's edge.

"Do you gentlemen mind if I take myself a quick bath?" she asked.

"Not at all," Slocum replied.

"Absolutely not," Barnaby added, licking his dry lips in a peculiar way.

"You gotta promise not to look," she said. "It's been two whole days since I had me a bath an' I can't hardly stand it when I feel dirty."

"We won't look, Miss Cass," Barnaby promised. "You have my word on it."

Slocum grinned. "I may take a peek every now and then, but you can't hardly blame a man for that. I won't stare too long, if that matters."

Nellie giggled, turning her back on them to unbutton what was left of the front of her dress. "I don't reckon a peek or two will matter all that much, Mr. Slocum," she said. "I've had men stare at me before."

She wriggled out of her dress, and contrary to Barnaby's solemn promise not to do so, he stared at her with his mouth open.

Slocum admired the rounding of her hips, the smooth curve of her thighs and her slender waist, the subtle turn of her calves with just the right amount of muscle.

"Don't look now," she said playfully, tiptoeing into the shallows of the pool. "Wild Bill might not like it if you stared at me too long."

"Are you Wild Bill's woman?" Slocum asked, straightening up from his work with the bay's forefoot.

"I reckon," she replied, wading into water that touched her knees, her back still turned to them. "Only, he's got more'n one woman."

"It looks from here like you would be enough for any man," Barnaby said, his face pinker than before.

Nellie glanced over her shoulder. "You promised me you wouldn't look, Mr. Watson. How come you're standin' there gazin' at me?"

"I'm sorry," Barnaby answered. "I suppose I couldn't help myself when I saw how pretty you are."

"That was a nice thing to say," she told him, bending over to cup water in her hands, dribbling it down the front of her body. "Most men I'm acquainted with don't say nice things to me."

"They should," Barnaby said earnestly, his eyes round as they roamed over her figure.

Slocum listened to the exchange with mild amusement. It was clear Barnaby had designs on the girl . . . and if he had the price, which he surely would if he were a successful drummer, he could most likely purchase lovely Nellie's charms for half an hour or so.

"You won't mention what I said to Marshal Hickok, will you?" Barnaby asked. "I wouldn't want to have a man like him angry at me."

"He wouldn't care," Nellie said, her voice softened by a sad note.

"Surely he would ... if a stranger told you that you were very pretty."

"Nope," Nellie assured him, continuing to bathe herself in the pool. "Bill don't really care 'bout women all that much. Only when he needs one."

"How terrible," Barnaby said. "A beautiful young woman like you should have someone who cares for her ... in the proper way, of course."

"You mean, like givin' me money?"

Now Barnaby was flustered. "Not exactly. That is not what I meant to imply ... that a man's feelings could be measured by the amount of money he gave a woman."

"Money's nice," Nellie said dreamily, looking up at the sky for a time. "Trouble is, seems like all my life there just ain't never been enough of it to go around."

Slocum asked, "Were you very poor when you were growing up, Nellie?"

"Dirt poor. There was eight of us kids. My pa run out on my ma an' she couldn't feed all of us on a wash-woman's wages, so I run off with a seed salesman. He swore he'd buy me new dresses an' shoes if I went with him."

"A seed salesman?" Barnaby exclaimed, like he knew a thing or two about seed peddlers.

"Yeah," Nellie replied. "He was a damn liar, too, a real good one. I was only fourteen."

"He didn't buy you any dresses," Slocum remarked, knowing the answer. "No shoes, either."

"He sure as hell didn't! He buck-jumped me in the back of his wagon for a whole week, an' never bought me a thing besides peppermint candy."

"What a shame," Barnaby said, paying closer attention when Nellie made a half turn in the pool that allowed him to view an outline of her breasts. "He sounds like a reprehensible scoundrel to me."

She looked at him. "I ain't sure what that means, exactly, not the first word you said, but he was damn sure a scoundrel, an' a liar to go with it."

Slocum liked the round firmness of Nellie's youthful breasts and he felt a slow warmth spreading through his groin. "Maybe it's time you kept company with a different breed of men," he said, with someone particular in mind.

4

Hickok was fuming, pacing back and forth in front of a window at the Bull's Head Saloon looking out on Texas Street. The heat in northern Kansas this time of year was all but unbearable, and now dry winds had begun to blow from the southwest for more than two weeks, sending clouds of alkali dust over the cattle town that settled over everything like a bride's wedding veil.

"What's eatin' on you, Bill?" Ben Thompson asked, proprietor of the infamous drinking establishment, where more bloodstains appeared on the floor than stains from poorly aimed tobacco juice meant for spittoons. The ceiling was riddled with bullet holes, put there by celebrating cowboys in years past, and when it did rain, an infrequent event, the Bull's Head Saloon leaked like a sieve.

"That damn little whore," Hickok muttered, his leathery face twisted in a grimace. "That rotten, no-good little blonde crib whore."

"You talkin' about Nellie?"

"Damn right I am. The bitch ran off with a bunch of cowhands up from down in Texas. Dave Boyd told me

25

he saw 'em ride out together . . . four of 'em, and she was with 'em, the sorry bitch."

"How come one little bitty whore is so special to you, Bill?"

"She ain't. Ain't none of 'em special, only I got to where I liked her. Not all that much, but you know how a man can get attached to a starving alley cat sometimes. I liked her more'n most of them others. Seems I made one hell of a big mistake to trust her. I shouldn't have ever allowed myself to get fond of the bitch."

"On account of she's so young . . . an' so damn pretty when she's fancied-up? You ain't never told me before, but just how old is Nellie?"

"Eighteen."

"That's powerful young for a woman to know her own mind. If I was you I wouldn't take it so hard that she run out on you. A girl so young ain't got no sense. Hell, ain't hardly any women got no sense. You're gettin' yourself all riled up over a damn soiled dove."

"I'd beat some goddamn sense into her head if I knew where to find her. She owes me eight dollars. Eight dollars, Ben. I gotta kill sixteen stray dogs in this shithole town to earn back that money."

"Did she buy a new dress with it?"

"Hell no. She was fixin' to be thrown right out of Maude's boardinghouse because she couldn't pay her rent. I loaned her the damn money so she could stay, and then she up and runs out on me with four cowhands. I shoulda knowed better. She wasn't nothin' but a damn whore in the first place, and a man in his right mind don't trust no whores."

"Ain't that just like a woman? Could be it wasn't her idea, Bill," Thompson suggested, as he wiped clean glasses on a shelf behind the bar. The place was empty, it being so early in the day. "Maybe they took her. Could be she didn't want to go off with 'em at all."

"Not likely. She was always asking me for money and I bet those cowboys promised her plenty."

"Promisin' is one thing an' payin' is another. Maybe she'll be back before long. Have a drink on the house, Bill. You look plumb flustered, an' it's over a damn woman. You can't let a woman do that to you."

"If I ever see her again I'm gonna change the shape of her face some," Bill promised, sidling over to the bar for his free drink.

Thompson chuckled, pouring the marshal a glass of red wine. "There's some who say you've got more women than one man can handle. You've earned yourself quite a reputation among the ladies in this town, Bill."

Hickok took the wine and gulped it down. It was noon, and already he was needing a strong drink. His cravings were coming earlier in the day now and he wondered if there would come a night when he'd had too many, enough so some young gunslick could slip up behind him and shoot him down unawares. "A man can't have too many women, Ben," he said. "Two or three spares is hardly enough some nights, if a man is feeling rowdy . . . even if they are whores."

Thompson chuckled again. "Damn, Bill. You've got one hell of an appetite for women, an' you ain't exactly a spring chicken in the age department."

"I'm young enough to pull my share of the load," he replied, pushing his empty glass in front of the saloon owner, a silent signal that he needed a refill . . . on the house, as was custom for the city marshal when he looked the other way over city ordinance and license violations. He and Ben Thompson had been friends for years and they knew each other well. Hickok knew just how far he could push him.

Thompson poured more wine. "Quit frettin' over Nellie," he said tonelessly. "Soon as them four cowboys run out of money, she'll be back quicker'n a wink. Just you wait an' see. I know a thing or two about women myself. When a man's poke runs dry, a woman will leave him quicker'n snuff makes spit . . . an' you know damn well I'm tellin' the truth. A woman will run off from a dry well before she gets her clothes packed. You know damn well I'm right."

"You damn sure are," Hickok muttered, raising the glass to his lips. "If there's anything sorrier than a sorry woman I don't know what it is. I'd as soon have a skunk under my bed as a whore in it . . .'specially if she was like Nellie, that rotten little bitch."

"We've both had bad experiences with 'em. Some gents just get lucky at the draw. I never was lucky when it came to the females. Seems like every one I've had has turned out to be a double-crossin' bitch."

Bill nodded, agreeing with Thompson's wisdom. "A damn whorehouse ain't the best place to find a good woman, Ben. A feller oughta go to church if he's wantin' a good one for himself, only I never was inclined to listen to a helluva lot of preachin' to get what I wanted. Not when what I wanted was a woman to spend the night with."

"Churchgoin' women ain't nearly so inclined to hoist up their skirts or drop their underwear. It's all that gospel they listen to that changes their minds on it. I'd rather have a whore any day."

"Amen to that," Hickok said. "A man could spend the rest of his life beggin' a churchgoin' woman to give him what he needs and she's still liable to say no. I figure it's bred into 'em from when they're real young."

"We're of the same mind when it comes to front-pew womenfolk," Ben agreed. "A whore's a sight more honest when it comes to that sort of thing. You pay your money an' drop your britches an' that's the end of it. You ain't gotta promise to marry 'em or nothin' of the kind.

Bill turned to the window again, remembering sweet Nellie and her beautiful body. "If I ever get my hands on that bitch's neck I'm gonna choke some sense into her . . . an' I'm likely to shoot them four cowpokes who took her away from Abilene with empty pockets an' empty promises."

Ben's forehead pinched in thought. "That boy killer, John Wesley Hardin, he choked the hell out of Kate Starr the other night. Claude seen it for himself. He said Hardin was drunk as a fiddler's bitch an' he woulda killed her if Bear River Smith hadn't stepped in."

Hickok had heard about the incident. "Bear River best be real damn careful 'round Hardin, Ben. There ain't many men on this earth I'm afraid of, but Hardin's different. He's plumb loco. I ain't sayin' I'm scared of him, mind you, but I damn sure wouldn't want to test my draw against him."

"He came up with the Clements herd, only he stayed on to be with Kate. He's a wild one, all right. Mean, too. If you can believe the stories about him, he's already killed more'n thirty men down in Texas."

Bill shrugged. "Them stories get all blown up, Ben, like the ones about me. I told this feller Stanley from back East, a damn newspaperman, that I'd gunned down a hundred men, and that didn't include Injuns. He printed every word just like it was gospel. The damn fool didn't have no idea I was funnin' him at the time."

Thompson lowered his voice, resting his elbows on the bar. "Tell me the truth, Bill, about that bunch up in Nebraska. I hear tell none of 'em was armed."

Hickok grinned. "It was this family of settlers. The

old man reached inside his coat like he was goin' for a gun. Hell, I couldn't just stand there. I shot him down, an' when his boys come at me lookin' for revenge against what I'd done to their pa, wasn't much I could do besides kill 'em all. I killed every damn one of 'em."

"Then they *didn't* have no guns."

Bill took a deep breath. "That's all I'm gonna say about it, Ben. Right then, with things happenin' so fast, I didn't have time to ask 'em if they was armed or not. They came at me like they meant to kill me. What the hell else was I supposed to do?"

Thompson seemed satisfied. "I've got the same problem down in Texas, in Austin. I killed one of the Bell brothers, only he didn't have no gun when he called me out on Sixth Street. He was drunk, so I shot the son of a bitch when his hand went inside his coat. Then I had to kill his younger brother, Dan, when he came to settle the score. Dan was carryin' a .44 out in plain sight, so there wasn't no argument about it. I let him reach for his gun first."

Hickok raised an eyebrow, reading Thompson's face. "You ever wonder if the day's gonna come when you'll be just a bit too slow?"

"I don't stay up nights worryin' about it. When a man's time is up, there ain't much he can do to stop it. But the older I get, the more careful I am when I cross a dark alleyway at night. My eyes ain't as good as they used to be, an' I don't hear so good, neither."

"I know the feeling," Bill agreed. "All the same, if I ever set eyes on them cowpokes who took Nellie off with 'em, I swear I'm gonna kill 'em. Every last one of the sons of bitches, for taking my woman out of town."

Thompson added more wine to Hickok's empty glass. "I never let a woman goad me into a fight. I get into enough of 'em the way it is."

"All the same," Hickok said softly, "if I see Nellie back in town with some other gent, I'm gonna plant his ass on Boot Hill, don't matter what his excuse might be."

A breath of wind swept through an open doorway at the back of the Bull's Head. Thompson wrinkled his nose over a stale odor and gave him a stare. "How come you pile all them dead dogs in back of my place?" he asked. "Looks like you could find a better spot."

"It's where Mayor Holt said to put 'em, Ben. Wasn't my idea at all. He said he could count 'em better that way, if they was all in one place."

"But why in back of my place?"

"You'll have to ask the mayor. Those dogs are worth four bits apiece to me, so don't go hauling any of 'em off 'till they get counted."

"Stinks worse'n hell."

"Can't help the smell, Ben. It's up to Mayor Holt where I put 'em after I shoot 'em."

"It don't seem fair. My customers have been complainin' about it."

"Tell it to the mayor. I gotta make a living durin' the off season."

"There ain't nothin' smells worse than a dead dog after it's been layin' there for a week. I have to keep the back door shut at night."

Hickok grinned. "A trail hand who wants a drink of whiskey bad enough don't mind the smell of a few dead dogs. The cowboys up from Texas have been smellin' cow shit for three or four months, so I don't figure they'll complain all that loud. Most of 'em ain't got no sense anyhow."

"But they can smell, Bill. Ask the mayor if you can pile 'em up someplace else."

Hickok nodded as Ben poured him yet another glass

of wine. "I'll see what I can do, Ben, only I can't promise you a damn thing."

Ben put the bottle away, to tell Hickok that his free drinks were at an end. "It's gonna be a long winter. I'm gonna close down next month an' head back to Austin until early in the springtime, when the herds start comin' in. You can do whatever you want with them dead dogs while I'm gone, but I'd sure as hell be obliged if they wasn't here when I get back."

Hickok drained his wineglass. "I told you I'd do what I could about it, Ben. Meantime, if you see that little bitch of mine named Nellie, you tell her she's got an ass-whippin' coming from me if I ever see her again."

"I'll deliver your message," Ben assured him. "But don't you go an' count on seein' her again. I figure she's gone to Texas . . . an' she won't be comin' back."

5

Ray Staples had grown tired of listening to Cole talk about the stranger. "Shut the hell up, Bob," he said. "If you're so damn mad about it, turn your horse around an' ride back to the creek so's you can shoot the son of a bitch. All you done so far is talk."

Bob Cole reined his horse to a halt. "That's damn sure what I'm gonna do, Ray. You in with me?"

"Hell no. I'm headed for Texas. Ain't seen home for nigh onto three months."

Cole turned to Deke Mason. "How 'bout you, Deke? Is you as yeller as these other boys?"

Deke gave Shorty Russell a sideways glance, for it was Shorty who knew about John Slocum. "It ain't got all that much to do with bein' yeller, Bob. All I'm tryin' to do is stay alive long enough to git home, like Ray."

"I say you sumbitches are yeller."

"That ain't my favorite color, Bob. Don't you go to callin' me no yeller bastard. Down deep, it don't set real well with me anyhow. I ain't yeller, or no kind of son of a bitch."

"If you ain't, then how come you won't ride back with

me to that creek so's we can git the woman back an' kill that sumbitch named Slocum?"

Shorty rested his calloused palms atop his saddlehorn, looking south, in the direction of Texas. "John Slocum's gonna be a real hard man to kill, Bob. If'n I was you, an' wanted to see my next birthday, I'd leave that big mean bastard plumb alone."

"He don't look all that mean to me."

"Maybe you need spectacles," Shorty suggested, sounding very sure of himself.

Cole raised one eyebrow. "You mean you've gone an' turned yeller on me, too?"

"My mama didn't raise no goddamn idiot, Cole. I didn't set out on the Chisholm lookin' for no coffin with my name carved on a plank above it."

"He's just one man," Cole argued.

"Maybe," Shorty agreed. "But one real tough hombre is as bad as ten of nearly any other kind."

Cole made a face. "You boys been up in Abilene too damn long, consortin' with whores, drinkin' too much of that rotgut whiskey."

"Maybe," Shorty said again. "Or it could be we ain't in the market for no bullets."

"To hell with all of you," Cole snapped. "I'm goin' back to fetch that whore, Nellie. I wasn't done with her yet, an' I damn sure ain't gonna take no bullshit from some bounty hunter I never heard of afore."

"That's the trouble with hearin' about a bad man, Cole," Deke said, rolling his cud of chewing tobacco to the other cheek. "By the time you know who the bad ones is, they've done killed you, or made you wish you was dead." He spat a stream of brown spittle into the dust beneath his horse, like he'd said his last word on the subject.

Cole's face became an angry mask. "I figured I came up this trail with boys who had some backbone. Turns out I was damn sure wrong."

"No need to say shit like that, Cole," Ray told him, turning his horse to the south. "We didn't bargain on no damn bounty hunter playin' his cards in this hand. We took that whore away from Bill Hickok, an' that was dangerous enough to suit damn near anybody. Hickok's a killer, only he just happened to be real drunk the night we took her. Hickok's damn sure a dangerous man when he's sober."

"So is John Slocum," Shorty said. "I ain't all that sure which one I'd rather have lookin' fer me."

"I'm goin' back to git the girl," Cole said, reining his bay north. "That drummer don't know which end of a gun to put the bullets in, an' this Slocum feller, he don't scare me none at all."

Deke glanced over his shoulder at Cole. "You got any family close to San Antone?"

"How come you to ask?" Cole wanted to know.

Deke shrugged. "Just so's we can notify your next of kin, in case we don't never see you again."

"To hell with all of you," Cole snarled. "You let some damn drummer an' a drifter take our woman away from us. I only got to hump the bitch twice . . . an' that was when her hands was tied up so's she couldn't hardly move."

"Better'n none at all," Shorty suggested.

Cole gave Shorty a dirty look and dug his spurs into his horse's ribs. He galloped off across the flint hills, sending a cloud of dust into the sky behind him.

Deke wagged his head. "I sure hope Bob knows what the hell he's doin'."

Shorty watched Bob gallop away. "He don't know

what he's in for, Deke. Take a good look at Bob Cole, 'cause I figure it's the last we'll see of him."

"How come you know so damn much about this Slocum feller an' how he's good with a gun?"

"I've knowed some tough sons of bitches in my time," Shorty replied. "Odel Pickett tol' me once he'd rather be throwed in a nest of rattlers than tangle with John Slocum. Odel ain't no slouch with a pistol."

"He damn sure ain't," Ray agreed. "I was in Waco one time when Odel Pickett killed Billy Sims right out in front of the Cotton Palace. He let Sims go for his gun first. Can't say as I never seen nobody any faster with a six-shooter than Odel Pick-ett."

Shorty nodded. "That's what I'm tryin' to tell you boys about Slocum. He ain't no kind of gent to fool around with, no matter how good you figure you are at the quick draw. He's fast as greased lightenin'."

"Let's get the hell away from here before Cole tangles with Slocum," Deke said. "If Cole makes Slocum mad enough, he's liable to come after the three of us."

"Ain't no grass gonna grow under me," Shorty said, touching his horse with a spur. "I aim to be the first one of us to cross the Red River. There's plenty more whores where she came from, an' a man ain't gotta risk gettin' killed in order to hang onto her."

The three of them kicked their horses to a lope, riding due south through the heat of late afternoon.

Cole rode upwind along the creek. He was no damn tinhorn himself when it came to manhunting . . . he'd done his share of killing over the years. Keeping to the trees, he pulled his Winchester .44 rifle and sent a shell rattling into the firing chamber.

"If Lady Luck's on my side, they'll still be here," he

said quietly. Cole knew he could pick off Slocum with one clean shot from a distance, and the drummer wouldn't give him any trouble whatsoever, not with the little peashooter he carried underneath his coat.

He jerked his horse to a halt when he spotted their horses in the shade of the cottonwoods a quarter mile away. With the breeze in his face, his scent wouldn't give him away to their horses until he was close enough to be certain of his first shot. And the next, meant to drop the drummer.

Cole tied his horse off in the thickest trees he could find and began a slow approach toward the water pool. He could see the whore, Nellie, taking a bath, and she was completely naked out in the shallows.

"That rotten little bitch," he muttered, creeping closer on the balls of his feet. "She's puttin' on a show for 'em, only the show's damn near over."

He saw the drummer, Barnaby something-or-other, standing on the creek bank staring a Nellie's ripe young body. "Get a good look at her, you fat son of a bitch," he whispered. "It's damn sure gonna be your last."

Cradling the rifle near his shoulder, its hammer pulled back so it was ready to fire, he moved more slowly now, for he was almost in range. The trouble was, right at the moment he couldn't find John Slocum among the shadows or near the horses, not anywhere that he could see.

"Where are you, asshole?"

Placing each boot carefully on summer-dry grass, he made for a fork in a big cottonwood's trunk where he could rest the barrel of his rifle, making his gun steady, his aim perfect if he were to squeeze the trigger gently. He judged the distance to be just a bit over two hundred yards, an easy shot for a good marksman who took his time.

He came to the tree and tossed his hat to the ground, so his outline wouldn't show in the tree's fork. Resting the muzzle carefully between the branches, he waited for John Slocum to show himself.

I'll show Shorty who the really mean hombre is, he thought, with more than a little satisfaction. Slocum was as good as dead when he came down to the creek.

A rare willow tree on the far bank, of the kind from which the slender stream got its name, swayed gently in currents of hot dry air.

Where the hell are you, Slocum? Cole wondered, growing impatient. No matter how closely he examined every dark spot below the cottonwoods, he saw no sign of the bounty hunter, no movement.

He found Slocum's bay among the tethered horses grazing on short grass near the creek, proof that Slocum hadn't ridden on without the girl.

Maybe he's takin' a nap, Cole thought. That would be just like a cocky bounty killer type, to believe he'd scared Deke and Ray and Shorty and himself away from the girl with all his tough talk.

"Show yourself, you son of a bitch," Cole said in the softest of voices.

"You looking for me?" a voice asked behind him.

Cole froze, tensed, caught completely unawares.

"Don't bring that rifle around or I'll kill you right where you stand, cowboy."

Cole glanced over his shoulder. John Slocum stood only a few feet behind him.

"Don't try it," Slocum warned again. "I meant what I said about killing you."

"How'd . . . you get behind me?"

"Easy. But I suppose I've had way more'n my share of practice."

"You mean you'd shoot a man in the back?"

"That's damn sure what you aimed to do to me. That Winchester ain't propped up the fork of this tree for the sake of decoration."

"There ain't no bounty out on me. You've got no call to shoot me down."

"I figure Marshal Bill Hickok ain't too happy that you took his woman away."

"She ain't nothin' but a damn crib dove."

"I'll tell Hickok what you said, when I bring you in tied across your saddle."

"He'd have to charge you with murder."

"I'll swear you went for your gun first. I'll say it was self-defense."

"My pardners from Texas will say otherwise."

"I don't think they'll be saying much of anything. They're headed for Texas. Now, put the rifle down and take out your pistol real slow. Drop it on the grass. If you don't do things just like I tell you, you're headed for Boot Hill."

Cole pulled his Winchester from the fork of the tree and put it near his feet, never taking his eyes from Slocum's face, or the hand near the butt of his pistol. "You ain't even coverin' me with your six-gun," he said, straightening up, growing angry over the fact he'd been tricked. "I was sure you had a gun aimed at my back."

"No need," Slocum replied casually. "I could have killed you any time I wanted."

"Ain't nobody *that* fast."

"I'm giving you the chance to find out for yourself. My gun is holstered. So is yours. You can reach for yours whenever you feel ready."

Cole swallowed, remembering the tale one of his

pardners told about Billy Sims in the killing at Waco, and what Odel Pickett had to say about Slocum. But stories got better with each telling, especially when it came to gunfights.

"You're thinking about it, ain't you?" Slocum asked, not moving from a slight crouch.

"Damn right I am, you big bastard. I've got it figured you'll be a fraction too slow."

Slocum's easy grin had no real humor behind it. "Then make your play, cowboy. Let's see if you're as good with a pistol as you think you are—"

It was all the challenge Cole needed, and just the right amount of distraction while Slocum made his speech. Cole clawed for leather, jerking his Colt Peacemaker .44 free.

He saw a flash of bright light appear before his eyes, and felt a thud against his breastbone while the crackle of a gunshot boomed through the cottonwoods.

Cole staggered back, firing his pistol into the ground as he was driven over on his back as if he'd been struck by a sledgehammer.

Then all was darkness around.

Deke Mason halted his horse at sunset, glancing over his shoulder. "Bob ain't showed up," he said. "Maybe that Slocum feller got him."

"It was Bob's choice," Shorty protested.

"We was pardners," Deke replied. "We gotta go back an' help Bob, if it ain't already too late."

"You can go if you want, Deke," Shorty said. "Me, I'm headed for Texas."

"Me too," Ray said. "It ain't none of my affair."

Deke swung his horse around. "Then I'll go by myself," he said, jaw clamped. "I may not be no match for

Slocum at the fast draw, but I damn sure know how to ambush a sumbitch."

He rode off into the paling skies of evening toward Abilene. Ray and Shorty kept moving south, toward Texas.

6

Nellie had been quiet most of the afternoon, as had Barnaby. When they rode to the outskirts of Abilene, Slocum paid passing notice to the skyline or the scattered buildings erected upon a broad prairie. He'd been to his share of tent cities or mining camps and cow towns over the years and he was certain this one would be no different.

Nellie turned to him, clinging to the sorrel's back with her skirt hoisted high on her bare legs. She gripped the saddle horn with white-knuckled hands, as if riding a horse was something she feared or was unaccustomed to. "I almost wish I wasn't comin' back to Abilene," she said. "I never wanted to see this place again."

"Why's that?" Slocum asked.

"I feel like a prisoner here. I've been stuck in this town for nearly two years."

"A prisoner?" Barnaby said. "But you are now free of those evil men who tried to harm you. . . . thanks to Mr. Slocum, and what little help I gave him."

"It's this town, mostly," she said. "The cowhands who

come here are the worst part. They don't take baths an' they take a woman for granted."

"What is it about Abilene you don't like?" Barnaby wanted to know.

She looked down at her torn, ragged dress. "I can't make enough money to go no place else, I reckon. I'm stuck here for the rest of my natural life. Leastways, it's startin' to seem like it."

"Not necessarily," Slocum remarked, taking note of the empty cattle pens lining the railroad tracks on both sides. It was the end of the cattle drive season and he wasn't surprised to find the corrals empty. Hundreds of thousands of beeves left here for eastern markets during the early spring and summer. Abilene now looked almost deserted. Rows of empty cattle cars stood on rail sidings. Dust swirled around the vacant cow pens in billowing clouds.

"Just what did you mean by that?" Nellie wondered, her eyes on Slocum's face. "How come you said I wasn't necessarily stuck here? Sure seems like it to me."

"You can leave damn near any time you want. A railroad ticket don't cost all that much. For a few dollars, you can board an eastbound train and go to Chicago, or Kansas City, or most anyplace."

"It costs more'n I got. I don't have a few dollars. Just the three Mr. Watson gave me." She lowered her voice when she said it.

Barnaby stroked his chin. He had given Nellie three dollars to buck-jump her after Slocum killed Bob Cole. Slocum was busy covering the body with mounds of flint rocks to keep the vultures and wolves from feeding on the corpse. "Where would you like to go, Miss Nellie?" Barnaby asked.

"Damn near anywheres besides this place. It'll be a

long winter without no cowboys. I'll have a hard time makin' a living out of here."

"You may have a hard time making a living," Slocum agreed, "if you stay in the same. . . . profession."

"I know," she said, gazing down at her hands. "I wish I was able to do somethin' else an' forget all about my past. If you know what I mean. Working those cribs wasn't exactly my idea in the first place."

"I understand completely," Barnaby said. "Perhaps you'd like to accompany me back to Saint Louis? I would gladly cover your expenses."

She wagged her head slowly. "I been wishin' I could see California. I hear tell they've got big opera houses an' all sorts of theaters. I think I'd like to be a dancer, or maybe an actress. I'd rather go west. If I had a choice in the matter. I seen enough of this part of the country to last me the rest of my life. I've been dreamin' about becoming a dancer, or an actress on the stage in San Francisco. I saw a tintype of those ladies once. They wear the prettiest dresses. I just know I could dance at one of them fancy dance halls."

"It takes some training," Slocum said, as they crossed the first set of railroad tracks. "You'd need to go to school to learn how to become a dancer, or a stage performer. But if you wanted it bad enough, you'd make it."

"It costs money to go to school, an' Wild Bill ain't gonna give me any. . . . leastways not enough to get plumb to California an' go to dancin' school."

"There may be others who would help," Barnaby suggested, his eyes straying to the girl's ripe body.

"I've got to where I don't believe what a man says to me no more," she answered. "I been lied to so much I ain't got much faith in a man's word."

"All men aren't the same," Slocum assured her. "Some men will keep their word to you."

"Wild Bill sure as hell won't. He promised me he'd take care of me, only, when he gets drunk he forgets all about them fancy promises he made. He finds himself another woman an' acts like he don't even know me."

"What a shame," Barnaby said. "What you need is to meet a man who is honest in his dealings with women."

The main street through Abilene was all but empty. A few carriages and horsemen moved about, along with women and children on the boardwalks in front of larger stores and shops. The place had a forlorn look about it, as though most of its residents had moved away.

"Town looks nearly empty," Nellie said. "Bill's gonna beat the hell outta me soon as he finds out I'm back in the Devil's Addition. He'll say I run off with them cowboys, when it wasn't my idea at all."

"The Devil's Addition?" Slocum asked, grinning when he heard the name.

"It's where most of the saloons are, 'cept for the Alamo an' them fancy places. The rest is over on Texas Street where the cowboys gather after they hit town with a herd. Won't be but a few left . . . the cowboys . . . so late in the year, an' I still ain't paid Bill back for the money he loaned me. He's liable to kill me over it."

"He won't kill you," Slocum said. "I'll make sure he understands what happened to you."

Nellie frowned. "I been meanin' to ask you all afternoon, Mr. Slocum. Bob Cole was an honest-to-goodness bad man with a gun, an' you killed him so easy . . . so quick, so it must be that what the other cowboy, Shorty, said about you is true. You're a hired killer, ain't you?"

"No ma'am. Cole went for his gun first. He thought he was faster, until I proved him wrong. Wasn't any money involved in it."

She watched the outlines of buildings as they came closer to town. "He sure did turn a funny dark color after you shot him, Mr. Slocum. I've seen dead men. Strange, how his color was so different. Nearly purple. It gave me the chills."

"I've never seen a pretty dead man," Slocum said, eyeing a place on Main Street called the Drover's Inn, one of the largest hotels he could see in any direction. "How about the Drover's Inn? Is it a right decent place to stay while I'm here in Abilene?"

"The best," she told him. "Only it's kinda expensive. The big ranchers up from Texas usually stay there, an' it's where the cow buyers from back east come to talk business over the price of the herds."

"The food is good," Barnaby said.

Slocum felt his empty belly growl. "Then you've just made up my mind for me. I'll hire a room for the night at the Drovers's and give their food a try. I'm also gonna take a bath in their bathhouse, and get myself a haircut and a shave, if I can find a barber's pole."

"There's plenty of 'em," Nellie answered. "I'm gonna swing off when we get to Texas Street, so I can explain to Maude at the boardinghouse about what happened. I hope she ain't throwed my clothes out."

Slocum gave her a look. "After you stop at the boardinghouse to check on your things, would you join me for dinner at the Drover's?"

She smiled. "I sure would, Mr. Slocum." Then her smile faded quickly. "Only Wild Bill ain't gonna like it. . . . if he hears about it."

"We'll have to drop by the county sheriff's office anyway, Nellie, to tell him about what happened to you, and to Bob Cole back there at Willow Creek. You can turn that horse over to the sheriff while we're there."

"Did you hear what I said about Wild Bill, Mr. Slocum? If he hears your brought me back to town, he's liable to come gunnin' for you."

"I doubt it. You let me handle Marshal Hickok. I'll explain things to him."

"Bill ain't all that good at listenin' to what other folks say, sometimes."

"He'll listen to me," Slocum promised, as they swung up the main road through Abilene.

At a crossroads near the middle of town, Barnaby Watson stopped his mules and tipped his hat. "I'll be parting company with the two of you here," he said. "My business will take me to the clothing stores."

"Pleased to make your acquaintance," Slocum said, offering his hand.

"Likewise," Barnaby said, then he turned to the woman. "It was a distinct pleasure to meet you, Miss Nellie Cass. Perhaps we'll run into each other again while I'm in town, if you have no objections."

"None at all, Mr. Watson," Nellie said, smiling. "You was a real generous man."

As Barnaby was about to ride farther up Main Street, a voice came from a shaded porch in front of the Alamo Saloon.

"Hey, stranger!"

Slocum turned toward the bench where a cowboy in a battered black felt hat sat, whittling on a stick. "Are you talking to me, mister?" he snapped.

The cowboy stood up slowly, and Slocum could see the pistol belted around his waist.

"I sure as hell am. In case you didn't know it, that's Wild Bill Hickok's woman you got with you."

Slocum shrugged. "Not according to her. She says the two of them are only friends."

"You either gotta be a dumb son of a bitch, or a fool,"

the gunman replied. He strolled to the edge of the porch, folded his pocketknife, and stepped out into the street with a mean look in his eye.

"I'm neither one," Slocum told him, swinging down off his horse. "My mama wasn't no kind of bitch, and I damn sure ain't a fool."

The cowboy grinned, yet the grin did not reach all the way to his eyes. "If you've got any sense, stranger, you'll get rid of that whore right away. She belongs to the city marshal, Wild Bill Hickok."

Slocum squared himself, letting his bay's reins trail in the dust. "Nobody can own a woman, you ignorant bastard. Now take back them words or I'll make you eat 'em."

"You don't appear to be all that tough, stranger. It takes more man than you to make me eat my words, or back down from the likes of you."

Slocum moved toward the cowboy. At the same time, Barnaby Watson tipped his hat to Nellie and urged his mules away from the spot.

"A man can't always judge by appearances," Slocum said, as he took longer steps toward the gunman. "I'm giving you one last chance to apologize for what you just said."

The cowboy stopped in his tracks, his right hand falling near his gun. "An' just what the hell do you aim to do about it if'n I don't."

Slocum walked up to him, meeting him eye-to-eye. "I'll slap those yellow teeth right outta your mouth, asshole, and then I'm liable to make you eat 'em, one at a time."

"Maybe you don't know who I am, stranger. I'm Woodrow Stark. My friends, an' my enemies, call me Woody. Surely you heard of me."

Slocum noticed Stark's fingers curling near the butt

of his gun. "Did you say your friends call you Wood-pecker?" he asked, with as much sarcasm as he could muster.

Stark's eyes became dark pinpoints. "I'm gonna kill you fer that, you son of a bitch—"

As the words left Stark's mouth, Slocum swung a quick backhand across the gunman's face. The blow was so powerful it knocked Stark off his feet, sending him toppling over on his back in the middle of the road.

A trickle of blood came from the corners of Stark's lips while Slocum drew his pistol, aiming it down at Stark's head.

Stark tried for a smile.

"This will be the last warning I give you, asshole," Slocum growled. "If you ever cross my path again, or say one more goddamn word to me, I'll blow that sick grin off your face and send you to the undertaker's. You understand me, asshole?"

Stark nodded. "Yessir, I reckon I do. Sorry for what I said about you, an' the lady."

Slocum turned away and led his bay to the east, toward the section of town known as the Devil's Addition, with Nellie riding close behind him.

7

Hickok sat at a corner table of the Bull's Head Saloon on the east end of Texas Street, enjoying another glass of red wine. The Devil's Addition, as it was called by the Kansas Territory newspapers, was quiet, too quiet to suit a man who made his living from difficulties, settling disputes or putting rowdy cowboys in jail. His reputation depended on it, and as a man who lived by his reputation . . . some of it given over to gross exaggeration, he needed action of some sort to keep him in the headlines back east.

Ben Thompson stood behind the bar wiping smudges off shot glasses and beer mugs. The quiet disturbed him as much as it did the city marshal, for it meant the sin district was empty, without patrons. A man in the sin trades could starve to death if things remained this serene. Abilene had built its reputation on being a place where a cowboy could spend his earnings without going to jail for his inclinations, including thirst for strong drink and a desire for fallen women.

Or gambling, which was outlawed in federal territories, but given only a token slap on the hand by Dickinson County authorities, if the bribe money was paid promptly. It was a corrupt system of local government that made some men rich during the peak seasons. Officials looked the other way when their pockets were filled on a regular basis. But only when the big herds were in town.

"You need another drink, Bill?" Thompson asked, as the disk of red sun lowered to the western horizon, turning windowpanes on the west side of the clapboard building in the Devil's Addition a pale shade of crimson. Some called it "Devilstown," simply because of the red color it took on at sundown, when the skies took on the hues of the fires of hell according to Scripture, a part of ancient literature that was seldom heard in this part of Abilene. Bible verse was as unpopular here as a temperance march.

The real reason it was known as the Devil's Addition was the ready availability of various sin trades, the pleasures cowboys sought after three or four lonely months serving as shepherds to herds of longhorns.

Thompson did not need to repeat his offer.

"Yeah. Why not?" Hickok wore his usual garb: a buckskin shirt with fringe and Indian beadwork of Crow design, a pair of tight-fitting denims, and a sash around his waist. Two pistols, a pair of matching Colt .44s with walnut grips, butts turned backward, rested in notched holsters across his mid section. He wore stovepipe boots in need of blacking, and his hair hung well below his shoulders in tangled masses, the mark of a plainsman who seldom visited a barber's shop. He had the look of a grizzly bear after hibernation, some folks said, a description he rarely denied since it added to his legend, the image he enjoyed west of the Mississippi, enhanced by the stories he told about his exploits carried by magazines and newspapers along the Atlantic coastline.

Thompson reached under the bar and brought forth a bottle of French merlot. "Too quiet 'round here. I reckon I'll be headed back to San Antone for the winter. A man can't make a dishonest dime in Kansas when the snow flies." He chuckled. "Or an honest living either. When a businessman can't sell bad whiskey or the services of a whore, or interest a man in a game of monte or poker, he'd best move on to another spot where they ain't overlooked."

Hickok nodded. "A man could starve to death in this shithole this time of year," he said, casting a glance out a front window. "This place dies deader'n pig shit after the herds stop comin' in. It could be said about Abilene that this is a town only five months out of the year. The rest of the time it's a graveyard."

"This is a shithole any time of year, Bill, an' you know it well as I do," Thompson said, pouring a glass of wine for the marshal. "If a man wanted to find the highest number of men with low breeding an' poor character, he'd start in Abilene, Kansas, an' work his way west. This would be the best place to start if you wanted a tally of sorry sons of bitches—men who would steal the pennies off a dead man's eyes, or a widow's pension. Worthless men are nearly as thick as cattle in Abilene in the spring of the year."

"Amen to that. I'll have to make my living shooting stray dogs until early spring," Hickok replied, his voice thick with the effects of wine. "There's no money to be made shootin' card cheats or liars. All the Dickinson County commissioners will pay me for catchin' a horse thief is four dollars. Ain't hardly worth the trouble. I can make more money killing dogs, and there ain't but half the risk. Never saw a single stray dog carryin' a shotgun."

"How come you don't scout for General Crook no

more up in them western territories? Nebraska, or the Dakotas? Looks to me like it'd pay better than being city marshal of a dead town like this. Injun scalps is worth ten dollars apiece down in Texas, or in Arizona Territory. Seems like scoutin' for the army would be easier."

Thompson sauntered around the bar and brought Hickok his wine.

"No need," Hickok replied. "Them Injuns, 'cept for the Crows and Sioux, are done fighting us. We whipped their asses good."

"A damn shame," Thompson. "You fought yourself right out of a job, Bill. Shouldn't have killed so damn many of 'em to start with."

"They got in the way of my guns," he said, making a joke of it.

Thompson stared through a front window at Texas Street, all but empty now. "I reckon it's like killin' them stray dogs you've been doin'. If you kill 'em all, you shot your way out of a job. A man has to know when to leave a few—Injuns, an' stray dogs."

"At fifty cents apiece, I can't afford to leave any stray dogs in Abilene," Hickok remarked. "I never did get paid by the head for killing Injuns when I scouted for Crook up in the Territories."

Thompson sighed, turning back for the bar. "Not a helluva lot of difference in a stray dog an' an Injun, Bill. Ain't neither one worth the price of the gunpowder it takes to get rid of 'em."

"I'll agree to that, too," Bill said.

They heard running feet coming up Texas Street, the sounds of heavy boots thumping on dry ground.

"Wonder who the hell's in such a hurry?" Thompson asked, reaching under his bar for a sawed-off Stevens twelve-gauge shotgun with a ten-inch barrel.

Hickok leaned forward in his chair, peering through a window for a moment. "Looks like that gunslick from Missouri, only I forget his name."

"Woody Stark?"

"Yeah. That's him."

Thompson chuckled. "Hell, Bill, he ain't no gunslick. He fashions himself a shootist. I'd bet my half interest in this here saloon he couldn't shoot a pig stuck under a muddy gate if he was standin' right over it."

"He stays clear of me," Hickok said. "I never got to know him all that well. Never was the slightest bit inclined to get to know him any better."

"You ain't missed much," Thompson remarked. "Just another cowboy with a gun who talks tough."

Woody Stark reached the batwing doors into the Bull's Head and burst through. His eyes swept the room for a moment, until they fell on Bill Hickok.

"Marshal!" he cried, out of breath. "One of the sumbitches who took your whore is back in town. I just seen him a few minutes ago."

"My whore?" Hickok asked.

"Nellie. The real young one."

"Where is the little bitch?" Hickok demanded, stiffening in his chair.

"She's with him. I seen 'em just now, along with a drummer on a mule. They's headed this way."

Ben Thompson spoke from his place behind the bar. "Looks to me like your mouth's bleedin', Woody. You been havin' trouble with a bad tooth?"

Stark turned toward the bar owner. "Hell no. That sumbitch with Nellie busted me in the jaw."

"Busted you in the jaw?"

Stark nodded. "He damn sure did. When I told him he was with Wild Bill's woman, he swung down off his horse an' gave me a punch in the face. I didn't see it comin' or I'd have damn sure killed him dead—"

Hickok came to his feet. "You say Nellie was with this feller?"

"Seen her with my own two eyes, Marshal."

"Was she hog-tied?"

"No sir. She was ridin' this sorrel hoss, an' she kept on smilin' at this feller she was with."

"What's his name?"

"I didn't catch his name," Stark said, rubbing his sore chin and bloody lips. "He come at me real suddenlike. I was caught off my guard."

Hickok ambled over to the swinging doors, looking out on Texas Street. "I figure that means I'll have to kill the son of a bitch."

"He needs a killin', Marshal," Stark said. "He's a real cocky bastard."

Hickok smiled. "One way to take the cockiness out of a man is to put a bullet through him."

"I hope you kill him," Stark added.

"What does he look like?" Hickok wanted to know. "Tell me, so I'll know who to shoot."

"Real tall feller. Wears a flat brim hat, an' a gun tied low on his leg. Hair as black as a raven's wing, an' eyes to match. Mean-lookin' bastard."

Thompson spoke from behind the bar. "Have you been drinkin' this early, Woody?"

Stark wagged his head. "Nary a drop. I was sober as a judge when I seen this hombre."

"You still haven't told us what happened to your lip. Did you cut yourself shavin' this mornin'?"

"I already explained how it happened, Mr. Thompson. He hit me when I wasn't lookin'."

Hickok scowled, still watching the street. "You're right sure it was Nellie Cass who was with him, Woody?"

"No doubt about it, Marshal."

Hickok glanced over his shoulder, giving Stark a cold, hard stare. "I'm gonna go lookin' for 'em. You'd damn sure better be right."

Hickok pushed through the doors, standing on the boardwalk for a moment to allow his eyes to adjust to the failing light of evening.

"You want me to back you up, Marshal?" Stark asked, coming out on the boardwalk.

Hickok wagged his head. "Never did need nobody to back my play with a gun."

"He's wearin' a gunfighter's rig. Tied down real low on his leg."

"I don't give a damn if he has a pistol stuffed up his ass," Hickok answered, loosening his Colts in their holsters. "That may be where I stick that gun of his . . . unless he's got a real good explanation for being with Nellie."

Stark looked toward the center of Abilene. "If it's all the same to you, Marshal, I'd like to come along . . . just to see this feller get what's comin' to him."

Hickok scowled at a pair of horses moving down the street. A woman was riding the sorrel. "Just so you stay the hell outta my way when the shootin' starts. I'd hate like hell to shoot you accidental."

"You got my word on it, Marshal . . . only I'll be there just in case he gets the drop on you."

Hickok turned quickly, his face a twisted mask. "Nobody ever got the drop on me, so just wipe that stupid notion from your mind."

"Sorry. I was only offerin' to help."

"I don't need any help. Just make damn sure you stay out of my way when the shootin' starts or you could wind in a pine box alongside him, whoever the hell he is. Are you right sure you didn't catch his name?"

"He never said who he was. Swung off his horse an' come at me when I wasn't lookin' for it."

Hickok stepped down into the street, able to make out the two shapes more clearly now. "That's the trouble with most of you boys who think you know your way around a gun."

"What's that, Marshal?" Stark asked, when Hickok offered no further explanation.

"You forget to look for trouble when it's right in front of you. Now remember what I said. Stay the hell out of my way while I find out why Nellie's with this bastard . . ."

The man and the woman reined off Texas Street before Bill could get a good look at them.

"Must not have been them," he said. "Nellie would come to me, if it was her. It's early. Maybe they'll show up later on, after the sun goes down . . ."

8

Barnaby Watson tied off his mules in front of the Alamo Saloon, thankful to be rid of the company of John Slocum after what he'd seen earlier in the day . . . the cold-blooded killing as the two men faced each other. It was a sight he would always remember.

Barnaby's pack mule and saddle mule were both in need of attention, but for the moment his thirst for whiskey made him forget his animals' needs, along with a vivid recollection of the shooting back at Willow Creek that still made him queasy, the way Bob Cole looked after he died from a bullet. A corpse had a certain quality about it few men would forget, if they had any sensitivity.

He caught a glimpse of John Meeker sweeping off the front porch of his dry goods store, and Meeker saw him at almost the same time. They were old friends, and Meeker was a regular customer of Barnaby's during the busier seasons of the year in Abilene.

"Glad you're in town, Mr. Watson," Meeker said, as a deputy city marshal named Calvin Cobbs strode up with a shotgun balanced in his left hand, giving both men a polite nod as he climbed up on the boardwalk. He was young, scarcely able to shave on a regular basis.

Barnaby tipped his bowler to Meeker, one of his better customers who always paid in cash, since many of the prostitutes in the Devil's Addition spent their earnings with him on fine shoes and silk stockings, in addition to corsets and some of Meeker's best dresses shipped in from Saint Louis. "Glad to see you too, John," he replied. "I feel very lucky to be here, after what I've been through recently. It's been one hell of a rough day."

"Did you have troubles along the trail?" Meeker asked, halting the motion of his straw broom, a frown creasing his dark face.

"Troubles!" Barnaby replied indignantly. "I almost lost my life to some paid shootists and a bounty hunter— all over a woman, a prostitute by trade, who claims to belong to Marshal Wild Bill Hickok. You may know her. Not that Marshal Hickok lays claim to having only one woman these days. I've known him to have several."

"What was her name?" Meeker asked, as the deputy marshal slowed in front of them when he heard Wild Bill Hickok's name mentioned.

"Nellie," Barnaby answered. "She says her full name is Nellie Cass."

Deputy Cobb came to an abrupt halt on the porch in front of Meeker's Dry Goods Store. "Did you say her name was Nellie Cass?" he wanted to know. "An' who the hell is this bounty hunter who's with her? I need for you to give me his name an' some sort of description of him, so I can tell Marshal Hickok who she's with."

Barnaby glanced up and down the street to make sure no one else was listening, fearing what John Slocum might do if he put the law dogs on his trail. "Slocum," Barnaby said in a quiet voice.

The deputy thumbed his hat back on his head, frowning a bit. "Would that be John Slocum out of Denver? Big feller with dark black hair? Kinda tall, an' he don't say all that much when you talk to him?"

Barnaby nodded. "One and the same. We met up with each other down in the Nations and kept company for two days on the trail to Abilene. I had no idea he was a killer, or a man who hunted wanted men for a living. He seemed quite amiable when we first became acquainted. He was a jovial sort, until we ran into those men who were holding Nellie Cass."

Cobbs continued to frown. "He's also a detective for the Kansas an' Pacific Railroad Company, if I remember right. We got a notice from the railroad office that he'd be aboard one of the trains guardin' a payroll of some kind. That was a couple of years back, seems like. Never heard no mention of him bein' a bounty hunter, like you say. He rides shotgun for Wells, Fargo now an' then. He's one bad hombre to tangle with, accordin' to the stories about him."

"He's a dangerous man," Barnaby assured him. "He killed a gunfighter who had Miss Cass tied up by her wrists down at Willow Creek. Shot him dead with the first shot. He said he was going to report it to the county sheriff. I saw the whole thing, but I would prefer to stay out of it if at all possible. This Mr. Slocum frightens me."

"Did you actually see it? The shooting?" The deputy wanted to know.

"I certainly did. I was only a few yards away when Mr. Slocum gunned him down. It was scarcely even a contest between the two of them."

"Who was this feller who got shot by John Slocum?" Cobbs inquired.

"He went by the name of Cole . . . Bob Cole. Mr. Slocum covered his body with rocks beside Willow Creek following the shooting incident. He left him out there on the Kansas prairie to rot in this miserable heat. If you ask me, this Slocum is about as cold-blooded as they come. He barely blinked an eye when he shot down Mr. Cole, like it was an ordinary thing to do. He has no inner feelings whatsoever."

"Who went for his gun first?" Cobbs persisted, like it made a huge difference to the law. "Did Slocum draw first, or did this Cole feller?"

"Mr. Cole drew first. Mr. Slocum invited him to draw his pistol. As soon as Mr. Cole reached for his weapon, Mr. Slocum shot him down with one bullet. It was truly an awful thing to see."

"I'll have to tell Marshal Hickok 'bout this. He may want to ask you some questions, since Miss Nellie was there at the time."

"Of course," Barnaby said. "I'll be glad to give Marshal Hickok all the details, if he feels hearing it from me is absolutely necessary."

"Where will you be stayin', mister?"

"At the Bedroom Palace over on Texas Street, just west of the sin district."

"What's your name, mister, so I can tell Marshal Hickok who to ask for?"

"Barnaby Watson. I expect to be in Abilene for three or four days. Then I must be moving on to Dodge City. I hope I can book passage on a train for myself and my mules, even though it is late in the year for trains to be running to any of the cattle towns. Dodge City is a new part of my sales territory now and I must make a few introductory calls on the merchants there who handle buttons and fasteners."

"I'll tell Marshal Hickok who you are, an' where you'll be stayin'," the deputy said. "Best I go find him now, so he'll know about it, an' about Nellie. I'll inform him as to where you're stayin' while you're in town, only don't leave without telling the marshal about it. He's gonna want to talk to Nellie first."

"She's with Mr. Slocum now, Deputy. He said something about taking her to her boardinghouse over in the district, a place called Maude's."

"I know right where it is," Cobbs said. "Thanks for your time, an' the information, Mr. Watson. I'm real sure that Marshal Hickok will be obliged. Only I figure he'll want to talk to you."

As the deputy started to walk away, Barnaby added a final thought. "Please tell Marshal Hickok that I'd like to stay out of the matter completely, if I can. I wouldn't want a man like Mr. Slocum angry at me over some small thing I said about this incident."

"I'll tell him," Cobbs said, sauntering off toward the east and the rougher saloon section of town, the part known as Devil's Town.

When Deputy Cobb was out of hearing distance, John Meeker spoke quietly. "You were very wise to ask to be left out of the marshal's personal matters, Barnaby."

"Why's that, John?" Barnaby paused on the boardwalk in front of the Alamo with concern creasing the skin across his forehead.

Meeker looked around him again, to make sure there were no listening ears close by. "When Wild Bill gets drunk he has this tendency to forget who his friends are. If I were you, I would not say any more about what you saw down at Willow Creek unless you're pressed for answers. Sometimes, in matters like this, it is best to remain silent unless you are asked for a specific answer."

"I understand, John. And thanks for the advice. I'm going in to wet my whistle at the Alamo for a short while. Would you mind keeping an eye on my mules and personal belongings for a few minutes?"

"I'll keep an eye on 'em, Barnaby. By the way . . . have you got anything new in the line of buttons? Something real colorful, if you know what I mean?"

"Just wait until I show you our new fall line of mother of pearl. You'll double your ususal order, I can virtually assure you."

Meeker scowled again. "I doubt it, John. This looks to be a long, slow winter for us."

"And why is that?"

"All them new cow towns springin' up at the end of every new rail line. All the action is over in Dodge City, accordin' to what I hear. We didn't get nearly as many herds in this spring as we usually do."

Barnaby straightened his string tie. "You *did* say most of the action is in Dodge City?"

"Right. It's a wide-open town. Marshal Wyatt Earp lets things go, unless they get too rowdy. Then he comes down with a hard hand."

"A hard hand?"

"He sends a bunch of lawbreakers to jail. Makes 'em pay big fines, too."

"I'll remember that," Barnaby said. "I appreciate the fact that you'll keep an eye on my mules and inventory while I'm inside wetting my whistle, John."

Meeker nodded. "Just don't be in there too damn long, Barnaby."

"And why is that, John?"

Meeker went back to his sweeping.

"You didn't answer me, John," Barnaby said again, letting impatience show in his voice.

Meeker glanced over his shoulder. "This town ain't the safest place to tie off no mules with a man's worldly goods tied to the saddle."

"But doesn't Marshal Hickok enforce the law and keep common thieves from robbing travelers?"

"Only when he's sober, Barnaby. You may have gotten here a bit late in the day."

"Dear me! Has Abilene become such a lawless place, so that a man can't trust the place where he leaves his belongings in the care of a friend?"

"We're only friends so long as you sell me the right merchandise at the right price, Barnaby. And even then, if any kind of trouble starts, I've got a family to raise. I can't afford to be fillin' no grave at Boot Hill over a few packsaddles full of buttons. You'll have to look out for your own . . . if there's gonna be any trouble."

"I'll remember that, John," he said, strolling toward the front doors of the Alamo Saloon with an uneasy feeling in the pit of his stomach.

9

Nellie swung her sorrel off Texas Street unexpectedly and led him toward a livery stable. The sun had dipped below the horizon and the western skies were ablaze with color—fiery reds and orange, lighter shades of pink, a painter's canvas for those who had an eye for such things.

"You can put your horse in that last stall," she said to Slocum, as they rode into the stable. "Unless you aim to keep that bay in a fancier place overnight. The Drovers has a real nice livery, only it costs fifty cents a night for a horse, a lot of money unless you think a helluva lot of that bay you've been ridin'."

"This will do," he said, swinging down from the saddle, inspecting the leather boot he'd made for the gelding. "I need to find a blacksmith first thing in the morning . . . to have this horse's shoe set properly."

"Where do you aim to spend the night yourself?" Nellie asked softly. "You asked about the Drovers—"

"I hadn't thought about it. The Drovers sounded like a nice place, according to Mr. Watson, and what you told me about it, and the food."

"It's the nicest place in Abilene."

"Then I'll repeat my offer. Join me there for dinner at eight."

Nellie began unfastening the cinch strap around the sorrel gelding. "I prob'ly can't. Bill will be lookin' for me, an' I need to make some money so I can pay him back the money that I owe him."

Slocum ambled over to her with his saddle and gear hanging across his shoulder. "I'll give you the money to repay your loan from Hickok." He reached into his pants pocket and handed her eight dollars in silver.

She stared up at him, quiet for a time. "What have I got to do for this money, Mr. Slocum?"

"You don't have to do anything, Nellie, but if you'd like to come to my room at the Drover's, maybe I can think of a way you can repay me. We'll talk about it over a nice, quiet dinner, if you like."

"I can't believe you'd trust me with this much," she said. "I just can't believe it. How come you give this to me when you don't hardly know me?"

"The money is yours, whether you come to my room at the Drover's or not. But you have to promise me that tomorrow we'll go to the sheriff's office, so you can tell him about the shooting between me and Bob Cole."

"I swear I will."

"I believe you."

"I've gotta pay Maude my back rent an' take a bath. I've got one good dress . . . it ain't got no holes in it. I'll come up to your room at eight o'clock, if that's what you want for this eight dollars."

"If you feel like coming," he remarked. "But you don't owe me a thing. You don't have to come to the hotel if you don't want to."

She smiled. "What if I do want to?"

"Then be there at eight."

She clutched the money to her breast. "You can count on it, Mr. Slocum. I'll be there."

He turned away to start back toward the center of town and the hotel.

Nellie spoke to him as he walked away. "I never met no man who didn't want somethin' for his money. You ain't like the rest of 'em, Mr. John Slocum. You may be a killer, or a bounty hunter, or whatever else they call you, but you're a gentleman at heart. I never had no man trust me before . . . not like this, not with eight whole dollars."

Slocum spoke to her over his shoulder. "Like I said, it won't matter if you decide not to come. The money is yours to keep either way. Just make sure my horse gets some oats and hay and a bucket of water. That's all I'm asking of you . . . that, and your promise that you'll go with me to the sheriff's office first thing in the morning."

"You got my word on it," Nellie said. "I'll be at your room as soon as I get myself fixed up. I won't be late. I'll be there before eight."

"I'll be in the bathhouse at the Drovers if I'm not in my room," he said, sauntering off, carrying his saddle, war bag, and rifle.

He didn't expect to see her again until tomorrow. As tired as he was, it made little difference to him now. Riding a crippled horse across half of Kansas Territory, and after the gunfight over a pool of muddy water in the middle of the Flints, he was ready for a bath, a shave, and a good night's rest. And a jug of sour mash whiskey to help him drift off to sleep, a thing he fully intended to purchase before he reached the Drovers Inn to hire a room.

•   •   •

He was relaxing in a high-backed cast-iron tub in the bathhouse behind the Drovers, enjoying pails of warm, soapy water brought to him by a chubby Mexican girl through a door at the back where kettles were on to boil.

He sipped from a bottle of Kentucky Red, tasting as sweet as mother's milk to a man who had been on the trail for days. And he puffed on a rum-soaked cheroot, the best he could find in this cow town, where fine cigars were rare. The finer things in life were scarce in prairie cattle towns . . . as was a woman a pretty as Nellie.

Slocum eased sore muscles back against the wall of the tub and rested his head there for a time. A Mexican woman, Consuelo, had given him a shave and a hair trim around the back of his neck while he was soaking. She'd been careful to avoid nicking his chin or cheeks, every now and then glancing at the holstered gun hanging from the back of a chair beside him. She seemed to be afraid of him for reasons he couldn't imagine, since he'd hardly said a word to her.

Every so often, he tried to begin a conversation with the woman.

"Tell me about Marshal Hickok, Consuelo. What do you know about him?"

She seemed reluctant to talk at first. "He can be a very mean hombre, señor. Sometimes, he can be nice to a lady . . . if the lady is young and pretty."

"So I've heard," Slocum replied. "I hear he has quite an eye for the womenfolk."

"Why do you wish to know?" Consuelo asked a moment later. "Are you maybeso in some kind of trouble with the law here in Abilene?"

"Nope. No trouble that I know of. I was only wondering about him, about what sort of feller he is. I've heard all sorts of stories about him."

"Very mean, señor. And very fast with a *pistola* if you make him mad."

"I hadn't planned to anger him. Just curious about what sort a man he was."

"If you pardon me for saying so, señor, it would be better if you stay away from him . . . especially at night. I should not be the one to tell you what to do . . . it is not my place to do this, señor."

"I hear he's bad about gettin' drunk. That's when he's the most dangerous. Somebody who knows him told me that not too long ago."

Consuelo nodded. "It is *verdad*, the truth, señor. When he is drinking, he is like a mad bull. He is not afraid of anything *en el mundo*."

Slocum drank more whiskey, then he blew cigar smoke toward the ceiling of the empty bathhouse. Since it was late in the year, he had the place to himself. "Somebody also told me he shot one of his own deputies . . . some kind of disturbance one night. I only heard the story recently, but I was surprised to find out he'd shot down one of his own deputies during some sort of local problem."

"It is true," the woman said softly, glancing over her left shoulder. "Marshal Hickok say it was an accident . . . that it was too dark to see, and Deputy Williams ran up behind him when he wasn't expecting it. That is what Marshal Wild Bill tell the people here."

"You sound like you don't quite believe that story, Consuelo."

She picked up her empty buckets and started for the back door. "It could be dangerous for me to say any more, señor. I do not want trouble with Marshal Hickok. If he gets mad at me, he can make life very difficult for me here. He is, as I told you before, a very dangerous man when he uses his guns . . . when he is drinking too much."

"Sounds to me like he *does* have everybody scared of him. I never knew of just one man who could be that tough, no matter who he is."

Consuelo left Slocum alone with his thoughts. Unless he'd badly misjudged Bill Hickok, Hickok was running on bluff here in Abilene, and probably an old, blown-up reputation he did not deserve, handed to him by some reporter from back east who was looking for an exciting story to tell his readers.

It was the way with many of the so-called Wild West characters he'd known over the years—mostly big talk about events that had not happened the way they were described in eastern magazines and newspapers—stories meant for readers with little regard for the facts of the matter.

Slocum heard the thump of heavy boots coming down the planks toward the bathhouse. As a precaution he reached out of the tub and drew his pistol.

A cowboy in rumpled clothing came into the bathhouse and when he saw Slocum, he stopped.

"You be Mister Slocum?" he asked.

"Depends on who wants to know."

"Name's Grimes. Wesley Grimes."

"What business do you have with me, Mr. Grimes. I don't believe we're acquainted."

"We ain't."

"Then why are you here?"

"To pass along a warnin' I heard outside the Bull's Head Saloon maybe half an hour ago."

"A warning? A warning meant for me?"

Grimes nodded.

Slocum lowered his Colt. "As far as I know, I don't have any enemies here."

"You got one," Grimes said.

"And who might that be?"

"A real bad enemy to have," Grimes went on.

Slocum grew impatient. "You still haven't given me his name."

"Hickok. City Marshal Wild Bill Hickok."

"I've never met him."

Grimes made a sour face. "Hickok ain't never met you either. He's been askin' who you was."

"And why is that, Mr. Grimes?"

"You rode into Abilene with his woman—the whore by the name of Nellie Cass."

"There is a reasonable explanation. I found her a prisoner of three cowboys south of town."

"Marshal Hickok don't believe it. He figures you're one of the men who took her out of town."

Slocum took a deep pull on his cigar. "Then it would seem I have to straighten Marshal Hickok out on a few matters—as to the way I met Miss Cass."

Grimes gave Slocum a critical eye. "I don't think you'll get the chancc to explain nothin' to him."

"I won't?"

"Naw. He's gonna kill you first, if he finds you in town tonight."

Slocum smiled a crooked smile. "Plenty of men have tried to kill me, Mr. Grimes. I'm still alive and kicking, as you can plainly see."

"You ain't never went up against Bill."

"That's true, although I never let a man's reputation scare me."

"You ain't never heard of Wild Bill Hickok?"

"I've read about him—"

"Then you've read how he's the fastest gun in this whole part of the West."

"I've heard that said about a lot of men."

"But wasn't none of 'em fast as Hickok."

Slocum rested his head against the back of the tub. "Being fast isn't enough, sometimes."

"What the hell do you mean by that, stranger?"

"Real simple—"

Grimes scowled, shoving his hands deep into his pants pockets. "I ain't followin' you. Maybe you had too much of that whiskey."

"It's simple," Slocum replied. "It does not matter how fast you draw a gun . . . it's what you can hit with it after you've got it in your hand."

10

Bill Hickok sat at a table listening to T. C. Henry read from a newspaper. They were drinking wine inside the Bull's Head at eight o'clock. Hickok was wearing his badge, and his brace of Colt pistols with the butts turned forward. Henry, Chairman of the Dickinson County Protective Association, had been elected by a vast majority of residents with a mandate to hire a new county sheriff who could enforce the anti-gun ordinance in Abilene and bring peace to the rest of the county. A former sheriff, Bear River Tom Smith, had recently been executed by a drunken visitor who chopped off his head with an ax. A man by the name of Roy Butler reluctantly took his place this past winter. He spent a great deal of time out of the county, fishing, many of his detractors claimed.

"Here's what the *Dickinson Herald* has to say, Bill," Henry said, after pushing his spectacles farther up his nose. "Hell is now in session in Abilene with the arrival of the big herds up from Texas this spring. Murder, lust, highway robbery, and whores run the city day and night. Seventeen souls snatched from this earth in less than a month, seventeen souls taken in their sins, ushered be-

75

fore their God without a moment's warning, and all this done at our county seat. Action must be taken, for we are fast becoming known as the meanest hole in the Territory! We must rid ourselves of these ruffians. The council has passed ordinances prohibiting firearms, fining prostitution, and requiring licenses for saloon keeping and gambling, yet signs announcing the prohibition of firearms posted at the Abilene city limits have been shot full of holes by drunken cowboys. Let there be a hue and cry from decent citizens to bring law and order to Dickinson County, and to Abilene in particular. City Marshal Hickok apparently has no interest in seeing our ordinances enforced."

Hickok took it all in stride, for he knew from whence his bread and butter came. "You don't really want me to enforce a policy of locking up these drovers, do you? Fining whores to put them out of business? Closing down gambling parlors and saloons without current licenses? Hardly a drinking or gaming establishment in town would remain open. Word of this would spread down the cattle trails like a prairie fire and the cowmen would turn their herds toward Dodge or Newton. Cowboys three months on the trail expect pleasant diversions. If we do not provide them, you should expect to preside over a dwindling town . . . perhaps soon a ghost town."

Henry sighed, nodding once before he put down his newspaper. "On the subject of outlawry, Bill . . . have you any ideas regarding who might be behind this band of cutthroats robbing trail hands after they leave Abilene to head home?"

"I'm a city marshal, T. C. No one admitting to being a robber has shown himself in Abilene, as you know. These men appear to prey on victims less likely to be able to defend themselves while in remote areas. If the

Protective Association could afford to put fifty deputies in the field, it still would not be enough to patrol every mile of the Territory at all hours of the day and night."

"But who do you think is behind these holdups? It's giving Abilene a bad name. Most of the drovers who've been robbed are nigras, or Mexicans. That, in itself, sounds mighty strange to me. Who's doing it?"

"I have no idea. Someone who is clever, very careful where they pull a robbery. Their methods may indicate some association with the Ku Klux Klan, although I rather doubt it. The Klan is not, on the surface, in the business of outlawry as far as I know. I know even less about the secret order of the Knights of the Golden Circle, a similar group that belives in the superiority of the whites. It may be that someone wants us to believe there is an association with one of these organizations." Hickok smoothed his shoulder-length hair for a moment, thinking. "If I were appointed sheriff of Dickinson County, at a substantial raise in pay, I might be able to get to the bottom of it. At present, my duties limit my authority to this township. I have no wish to interfere in Sheriff Butler's affairs. I'm sure you understand."

Henry looked askance. "There was the problem with Mike Williams, Bill. You accidentally shot one of our own policeman over that dog incident. Folks still remember it. Makes it hard to get you the appointment to county sheriff, with that fresh in everyone's mind."

"It was dark, T. C., and I was surrounded by an angry mob of at least fifty men. Mike rushed up behind me, startling me, and I was too quick to pull the trigger. Mike was my friend. I am still saddened by what happened that night."

"I do understand, Bill, however there are some among the councilmen who believe you are a bit too trigger-happy. It may be difficult to get you that job."

Hickok's irritation was growing. "I'm asked to control a wide-open town, where gunshots are the order of the day. But when I meet violence with violence, I am soundly criticized. A huge majority of local businessmen want things left as they are, for fear of losing the cattlemans' trade. I see nothing wrong with an occasional shooting when a particularly rowdy cowboy is threatening the lives of others. Some of our troublemakers are professional gunmen and gamblers. I tolerate them, so long as they don't go too far. But as you know, I've killed a few and it serves as notice that there are limits."

"I know, Bill," Henry said. "You have your supporters as well as your detractors. Personally, I think you've done an admirable job. As this newspaper says, hell is in session in Abilene from spring till the end of the summer. I promise to do whatever I can to get you that appointment to county sheriff, but it may not be possible."

"At a significant increase in pay, T. C. Last month I made more money shooting stray dogs for fifty cents apiece than I did from my city marshal's salary. The stray dog ordinance has seen me through the winter."

"You should enjoy a substantial increase in fines early next year, when the cattle herds are arriving."

"My small percentage of fine revenue is appreciated, but it puts me at odds with the businessmen I'm sworn to protect. If I lock up too many of their customers—" He was interrupted by a shout coming from a young cowboy rushing through the batwings.

"Marshal Hickok! I found a fresh grave down at Willow Creek, an' the cowboy buried in it is Bob Cole. I've known Bob for years."

Hickok turned in his chair as the freckle-faced cowhand ran up to his table. "Where did you find the grave, son?"

"South of town . . . maybe five or six miles," he gasped, out of breath.

Hickok gave T. C. Henry a glance. "It's out of my jurisdiction," he told the drover. "You'll have to find the county sheriff, Roy Butler. I'd imagine he's home in bed at this hour. Or he may have gone fishing."

"Yessir, Marshal Hickok. Can you tell me where he lives?"

Hickok shrugged, lifting his glass of wine. "Let me introduce you to Mr. T. C. Henry of the Dickinson County Protective Association. He'll be glad to give you directions to Sheriff Butler's house . . . but watch out for that dog of his. It's known to bite strangers on a regular basis. I almost shot the creature once, when it got off its chain. I would have earned fifty cents, had I chosen to do so."

The cowboy gave Hickok a strange look, even though the terror of his recent incident when he discovered the new grave still showed in his eyes. "You make fifty cents for shootin' dogs?"

"Loose dogs are in violation of a city ordinance. The same goes for that gun you're carrying. If I were to enforce all our city ordinances to the letter, I'm afraid I'd have to put you in jail right now."

"Are you gonna, Marshal?"

Hickok enjoyed T. C.'s obvious discomfort. "I could be branded a crooked lawman if I made any exceptions."

"I didn't see no sign or nothin'. It was dark."

Hickok smiled. "Mr. Henry will give you directions to the county sheriff's residence. The sheriff will look into this affair . . . but remember to watch out for that dog of his."

Roy Butler was dressed in his nightshirt. The constant barking and snarling of his pit bull brightened lanterns behind several windows in the neighborhood. Tonight, the black dog was on a chain, a fact that had probably saved a cowboy up from Texas a number of stitches in his leg.

Dave Dunlap stood on the front porch with his hat in his hands.

"What the hell is it you want, son?" Butler asked, lowering the twin barrels of his shotgun when he got a better look at the cowboy. He had jerked his front door open, ready to shoot at the first target he could find if he did not recognize the man who was doing the knocking.

"There's been a killin', Sheriff." The boy said it in a solemn voice, eyes downcast.

"That ain't big news in Abilene. Did you see who done the shootin'?"

"No sir."

"Then how come this bit of information couldn't have waited till morning?"

"I found this grave, Sheriff."

Butler made a face. "Hell, boy, Dickinson County is full of graves."

"It was real fresh. Like it had only been dug for a few hours."

"If it was in Abilene, the proper authority to handle it would be City Marshal Bill Hickok. You can probably find him down at the Bull's Head Saloon at this hour . . . if he ain't bedded down with some whore. Could be it's too early for him to take a whore to bed."

"I done talked to him."

Butler scowled. "And what exactly did Marshal Hickok have to say?"

"He said it was in your jurisdiction."

"My jurisdiction? How come?"

" 'Cause it was down on Willow Creek. Wasn't in the city limits of Abilene."

Butler rolled his eyes. "Just where on Willow Creek did you find this . . . fresh grave?"

"South of the crossin'. You know where the big herds come across"

"The crossin' on the Chisholm Trail?"

"Yessir. Right near where them big Willow trees grows next to the bank."

Butler fingered his shotgun. His duty as sheriff of Dickinson County demanded that he investigate any report of a killing, if that's what the grave meant.

"Sorry to wake you up so late, sir," the cowboy said as he fingered the brim of his hat.

"How did this feller die? Could it have been from the fever or natural causes?"

"No sir. He had this big bullet hole in him, right up next to his heart. Like I said, I'm real sorry to wake you up at this time of night, but I just knowed I had to report what I found to the law."

"It's okay, I reckon. Give me a few minutes to get dressed an' I'll saddle my horse, so you can show me just where this grave is located."

"I'll wait out by the front fence, Sheriff. That dog of yours damn near chewed my leg off when I come through the gate a minute ago."

Butler nodded. "That's why I keep that sorry dog around, so he'll be a discouragement to strangers. A man never can tell when some son of a bitch with bad intentions is gonna come on his property."

"I didn't have no bad intentions, Sheriff. Marshal Hickok told me to come. A dog who'll tear a man's leg off can be worth his weight in gold. I was just real careful to stay away from the end of his chain."

"I understand. Wait for me outside the fence. I'll get

some britches on an' saddle my horse. May take me ten
or fifteen minutes. If you found a grave with a body in
it, I don't figure the dead man is gonna run off afore we
get there."

"No sir, an' I'll be waiting outside the gate just like
you said."

Dunlap sauntered off the porch, again staying wide of
the end of the chain while the black pit bull continued
to snarl at him.

Roy Butler dressed by the light of a small lantern in his
bedroom. He heard his wife stir beneath the bedcovers.

"What is it, Roy?" she asked sleepily, stretching on
the mattress.

"Some damn drifter found a fresh grave down at Willow Creek an' wants me to investigate.

Edith Butler sat straight up in bed. "You know I don't
approve of no cussing inside this house, Roy."

"I didn't say nary a single cussword, dear."

"Yes you did."

He tried to remember what he told her. "You must
have been dreamin', darlin'."

"I wasn't dreaming when you said some 'damn'
drifter found a grave at Willow Creek."

"She had him cold. "Sorry, dear. He's just some
drifter. I was half asleep when I told you about him
comin' to the front door."

"That's no excuse for using profanity under the roof
of two God-fearing people, Roy."

"I said I was sorry. I was damn near . . . I was almost
asleep when he came to the door."

"Now you've gone and done it again. What would
Reverend Barnes think if he coulda heard you just now,
cussing a blue streak."

"I wasn't cussin' no blue streak, Edith. I was sleepy.

It looks like the good Lord oughta forgive a man who ain't woke up all the way."

"It's sinful behavior . . . like common street trash talks, an' you are a deacon at the First Baptist Church. You're supposed to set a Christian example for other folks to live by. May the Lord have mercy on your soul."

He pulled on his boots, wishing he'd never lit the lantern to dress. "I swear by all that's holy I'll ask the Almighty to forgive me on Judgment Day, Edith. Meantime, I've gotta go take a look at that grave. The cowboy's waitin' outside."

Edith fell back on her feather pillow. "I've married a sinner," she said bitterly. "My mother was right about you from the beginning."

He strapped on his pistol, turned out the lamp, and went quietly out the back door. There would be hell to pay when he got back from Willow Creek. Edith was sure to carry on about his cussing the rest of the week.

11

He had a bottle of peach brandy sitting next to the wash-basin in his room, more for the woman's sake than his own, even though it was unlikely he would ever see Nellie Cass tonight. After giving her the eight dollars in silver coins, Slocum was all but certain she would be in the Devil's Addition, looking for Wild Bill Hickok. Hadn't one of the cowboys at Willow Creek said she was Wild Bill's woman?

He was dressing, after his hot bath, haircut, and a shave in the bathhouse, when he heard a soft rapping at his hotel room door. He'd been planning on going downstairs to the cafe in order to get a bite to eat.

Slocum glanced at his father's old pocket watch, the one given to him by his dad before he went off to war. The time was a few minutes before eight. Sometimes, just looking at the watch brought back old memories . . . of his dead brother, other things he tried to forget.

He crossed over to the door, reaching for his Colt .44-.40 resting next to the washbasin and pitcher. His .32 caliber Smith & Wesson bellygun lay on the bed. He was rarely without it anywhere.

"Who is it?" he asked through a crack in the door, his thumb resting on the hammer of his pistol.

"Nellie," a soft voice said. "You told me to meet you here at eight o'clock."

Slocum was surprised. Holding the revolver behind his back, he slid back the latch and twisted the doorknob open very cautiously.

He found Nellie standing in the hallway, her hair done up in ribbons, wearing a pale blue calico dress.

He smiled when he saw her. "I didn't expect you . . . not quite so early," he said, stepping back to admit her. In his experience a woman was never early for an appointment, especially if she had been paid in advance.

"I had to hurry," she replied, coming into his room with the faint smell of lilac water in her hair. "Bill was havin' some men look for me. He's already heard I was back in Abilene, if what Maude over at the boarding-house told me was the truth, and I figure it was."

Slocum gave the hallway a glance to be certain it was empty before he closed the door behind Nellie. It always paid to be careful.

"I'm almost dressed," he told her. "All I've gotta do is put on a clean shirt."

Nellie was staring at his naked chest. "You've got big muscles, Mr. Slocum. And you sure do have a whole bunch of scars on you, too. How did you get so many scars on you? Why, it looks like you've been shot, or cut, all to pieces."

"Most of 'em came from the war," he replied, admiring the way her dress clung to her body in the heat. "I was lucky. I knew a lot of men who didn't make it back home after Gettysburg. Give me half a minute and I'll be dressed so we can go downstairs and get some decent food. And by the way, from now on, call me John. Mr. Slocum sounds too fancy."

She reached for his arm, touching his bicep with the tips of her fingers. "I took a bath," she said, "an' I hope you like my dress. It's the best one I've got."

"Maybe some feller should buy you a new dress," he said, as his voice thickened with desire. "The right man, if he was taken with you, might buy you several new dresses, and new leather shoes to match. It would be easy to see how a man could be taken with you, Nellie."

A tiny frown knitted her smooth forehead. "Bill won't buy me nothin' . . . not even a new scarf or a bottle of perfume. Times, I wish I'd never had nothin' to do with Bill. He can be real mean to me sometimes. When he's been drinkin' too much, or when he's in a bad humor over somethin'."

"A woman hadn't oughta stay with a man who don't treat her like a lady."

Nellie gazed down at the floor. "I reckon he knows I ain't no lady," she said softly. "A proper lady don't work the cribs like me."

"It wasn't your fault," Slocum said. "You told me about the traveling seed salesman, and how poor you were when you were a bit younger."

She nodded. "I did try to find honest work, only there wasn't hardly none to be had. Everybody I went to told me I was too young. I done laundry for a spell, until the lady who owned the laundry fired me one night while I was workin' late, boilin' shirts. Men kept tellin' me I was pretty, when they came to pick up their laundry, an' they promised that they'd give me lots of money if I . . ." Her voice trailed off as a tear came to her eyes. "I never intended for things to end up this way, only I just didn't seem to be able to stop what men had to say about me, or the way they looked at me."

"You are a pretty girl," Slocum said. "I figure it's only

natural that some men will tell you about it . . . about how good you look."

She looked into his eyes. "Do you really think I'm pretty, Mr. Slocum . . . John?'

"Very pretty indeed."

"Or is it that all you want from me is the same thing the others want?"

"The first thing I want to do is take you downstairs for a quiet dinner. After that, we'll just let events take their natural course."

"You mean you don't wanna buck-jump me for that money you loaned me?"

He took a clean shirt from his valise and put it on. "I didn't say the thought hadn't crossed my mind, Nellie. But right now, let's get something good to eat. All I want now is the pleasure of your company for dinner. Forget about the money I gave you."

She gave him a curious stare. "I don't believe I've ever met another man like you, John Slocum."

"And how's that?"

"You don't seem to have strong urges like most other men do."

He grinned. "Don't be so sure of that. Right now, I'm hungry. Before we go downstairs to the Drover's Inn Cafe, why don't you have a glass of peach brandy? It's good for stimulating the appetite."

She glanced at the bottle beside his bed. "I'm nearly starved to death anyway, but a glass of peach brandy sure does sound nice. I like the sweet taste of it and the way it makes me feel."

He strolled over to the washstand and pulled the cork on the brandy, pouring Nellie a generous amount into a smudged glass beside the washbasin. "Here," he told her, handing her the drink. "It won't hurt a thing to have a drink or two before we go downstairs."

She took the glass. "You sure are a nice feller, John," he said, tasting her golden brandy. "Oh my! That is nearly the most delicious taste of spirits I ever had in my whole life. It nearly tastes as sweet as honey."

"Take your time, Nellie. I'll have some brandy with you and then we'll find out if the food downstairs is as good as the brandy they sell around here."

She giggled while he poured himself a shot of brandy and tossed it back.

He slipped into his bib-front shirt and took a drink of brandy for himself, tucking his shirttail into his pants, then his bellygun so it was hidden, out of sight, keeping his back turned to the lady.

Platters of beefsteak, fried potatoes, and baked yellow squash sat in front of them.

"I never saw nothin' so beautiful before," Nellie said, as a waitress brought them long-stemmed glasses of red wine and dinner rolls made of sourdough, along with a bowl of butter and a red fruit jam. "I feel like a queen of some kind . . . I reckon maybe the queen of England."

"Enjoy your dinner," he said, cutting into his tender piece of sirloin. "After we eat, we'll order pie. Maybe some ice cream to go with it."

"I'll be so full I can't get out of this chair, John, if you buy me all of that."

He laughed. "Maybe later on, we can go for a stroll across town."

Nellie shook her head quickly. "That wouldn't be no good idea, John."

"And why is that?" he asked.

"Because Bill Hickok has folks out lookin' for me, now that he knows I'm back."

Slocum shrugged. "You worry too much, Nellie. If Marshal Hickok shows up, I'll handle things."

"Are you as mean with a gun as Shorty Russell said you was, John? You sure don't act scared of Wild Bill like any man oughta be."

He tasted his steak, finding it delicious. "I'm not afraid of any man, so long as he's standing in front of me where I can see him. Now, eat your dinner before it gets cold. You leave Bill Hickok to me . . ."

They ate slices of apple pie covered with vanilla ice cream and had two more glasses of wine each. Nellie ate like she hadn't been fed in a week, scooping up the last of everything.

"I'd be fat as a baby pig if I ate like this real regular," she said.

"Good food is to be enjoyed. Nothing wrong with splurging once in a while."

She seemed nervous now, as darkness blanketed the veranda around the Drover's.

"What's wrong?" he asked her, when their waitress carried their plates away.

"Just a bit worried, is all."

"Worried about what?"

"Bill. That someone he knows will tell him I'm here with you, and that there'll be trouble over it."

Slocum smiled. "I told you before . . . you let me worry about Marshal Hickok."

"You just don't know how mean-natured he can be over a woman he thinks belongs to him."

"A woman belongs to no man, Nellie. I assure you I can persuade Mr. Hickok to leave you alone while you are keeping company with me."

She glanced up and down the street in front of the Drovers again. "I'd feel more comfortable if we went up to your room for a spell . . . just to have another taste of that wonderfully sweet peach brandy."

"Consider it done," he said, signaling their waitress for the bill. "We'll enjoy a few drinks, and then perhaps go for a stroll, or a buggy ride, through Abilene."

She touched her lips with her linen napkin. "I've done told you that bein' seen in town with you would not be all that good an idea."

"You leave that up to me," he told her. "But first, I think we should have some brandy up in my room."

"That sounds nice, John. I do so enjoy your company, an' I want to thank you for a lovely dinner."

He paid the bill when their waitress returned and gave her a generous tip. "Let's go upstairs," he said, pushing back his chair so he could help Nellie out of hers. "The night is still quite young. Who knows what will happen later . . ."

As he was pulling back Nellie's chair, a cowboy with a mean set to his eyes stopped in front of the veranda surrounding three sides of the Drovers.

He stared at Nellie a moment.

Slocum ambled over to the railing across the front of the porch. He noticed Nellie's face had gone pale.

"Something catch your eye, stranger?" he asked.

The cowboy wearing the low-slung gun ignored Slocum's remark for the time being. "Is that you, Nellie?" he asked in a cold, grating voice.

Slocum did not give Nellie time to reply. "I asked you a goddamn question, you stupid son of a bitch!" he snapped, bending over the porch rail. "Is there something about the lady that caught your eye?"

Now the cowboy's beard-stubbled face was turned toward Slocum. "That ain't no lady, mister, an' unless my hearin's gone bad, you just called me a son of a bitch . . . a stupid son of a bitch."

Slocum watched the cowboy's gun hand move closer to the butt of his holstered Colt. "There's nothing wrong with your hearing, and I did call you a son of a bitch. A stupid son of a bitch at that." Slocum's palm was now very near the handles of his .44-.40 and he was ready for the gunman to make his play.

He heard Nellie's tiny voice speak behind him. "Don't do it, John. Don't tangle with this feller. He's Buck Smith, a real good friend of Wild Bill's."

"Never heard of him," Slocum snorted as he jerked his gun free of its holster, aiming squarely between the eyes of Buck Smith before Buck could begin to draw his gun.

Slocum cocked his Colt. "Listen to me, Buck Smith, or whoever the hell you are . . . this lady is with me, and as long as she's with me, she's a lady. I don't give a good goddamn who you are, or who you're friends with, but if you ever stop to stare at a lady who's in my company again, I'll kill you deader'n pig shit. Do you understand me?"

Staring into the muzzle of Slocum's .44, Smith nodded and backed away from the veranda. "Yessir, I sure do," he stammered, hurrying off down the street, turning toward the Devil's Addition.

12

He had taken her up to his room right after their dinner at the Drover's. She offered little in the way of resistance when he took off her dress and pushed her down on the mattress.

Then he took off his own clothing, hanging his gun from a bedpost.

Slocum lay naked beside her on the bed, the room's small oil lamp turned down to a tiny point of light after she had taken off his clothes. She poured herself another brimming drink while he took several swallows of brandy. Later, he'd pushed her over on the mattress tenderly, laying her head on two pillows. Nellie's breathing had grown faster. She stared into his face, caressing his cheek with her fingertips.

He kissed her lightly on the nape of her neck, and she sighed, the beginnings of pleasure. Her golden hair lay spread over the pillows.

"Your body is so hard," she said softly. "There isn't any fat on you. Only those scars . . ."

"I'm on the move pretty regular. It's hard to eat much when you live in a saddle so much of the time. The various types of business I'm in forces me to travel a lot, but I can't honestly say I mind it."

"You told me you buy racehorses. What else do you do for a living?"

"I work for the railroads some."

"You're an engineer or something like that? You don't seem the type. Those men said you were a bounty hunter."

He smiled. "I do occasional detective work, when some bunch robs a train. Train robbers are hard men for the law to catch, since they usually clear out of the country where they commit a robbery. Somebody has to follow 'em and bring back the company's money. Every now an' then a bank will hire me to find holdup men when a bank's been robbed. Mostly I travel. I like to see the parts of the country I've never seen."

"Working to chase down outlaws sounds dangerous. You must be very brave and good with a gun." The frown wrinkling her forehead said she was surprised by what he'd just told her about his various occupations and pastimes . . . and his lifelong case of wanderlust.

"I get by," he said. "Most men with bad reputations aren't really all that bad when the chips are down."

"Wild Bill is a coward, I think. I don't really know him all that well. He uses a gun when he's sure he has the advantage, or when he knows someone won't fight back. A few men who know him said he was extra good with his pistol in a shoot-out, but I don't believe he'd face someone like you."

"You don't know that much about me either," Slocum said.

"A woman can tell, if she knows anything about men."

"And you claim you do?"

She kissed his lips, moving her mouth over his. A low

moan came from deep in her throat. Her tongue flicked between his teeth, exploring. Nellie was finished with talking, evidenced by her actions.

Slocum cupped one ripe breast in his left hand and gave it a gentle squeeze, keeping her hardened pink nipple between two fingers.

She pulled her lips away from his. "Oh John. That feels so good."

His cock rose higher, until it touched the soft flesh of her abdomen.

"Dear me," she exclaimed, although she said it quietly. She dropped one palm down to his shaft, encircling it with dainty fingers. "Your body isn't the only thing you have that is very, very hard."

"Natural urges," he explained, "when I'm in bed with a real beautiful naked woman."

"It's so big." Her breathing quickened even more, her nostrils flaring with each breath.

"I'm sure there are plenty that are bigger."

"I've . . . never seen one."

He wondered how many stiff cocks she'd seen, more than a few, he supposed. But a woman with experience was far more satisfying in bed. Since the age of fourteen, Slocum had had plenty of both kinds, more than enough to have a deep appreciation for the difference.

Nellie began to stroke his prick, slowly at first, pulling his foreskin back and forth over his glans. He felt a tingling sensation spread from his cock to his groin.

"My goodness," she whispered, glancing down at the work she was doing with her hand. "It's getting even bigger . . . thicker. I don't see how."

"It happens when I see a woman I like," he told her. "Been behavin' that way since I was young." He grinned. "Sometimes it acts like its got a mind of its own."

She giggled, gazing into his eyes again until the mirth left her face. "You'll like me, John," she promised. "I'll be good to you, so good you'll never let me go, only please get me out of this town and away from Bill. I'm afraid he's going to kill me some night. He's mad because he knows I'm back in Abilene an' I haven't contacted him. I'm really scared he'll kill me over it, if he finds out I'm with you."

"I've already promised you I'd see to it that you were safe," he said, pinching her right nipple even harder. "Anything beyond that sort of depends."

"Depends on what?"

He kissed her lips again. "I reckon it depends on how well you perform in this bed tonight. It takes a woman with know-how to satisfy me."

"I can do it," she whispered, a plea in her feathery voice while she continued to stroke his cock, moving her hand faster up and down the full length of his shaft. "Just don't leave me here in Abilene where Bill can get his hands on me."

He noticed a tremor in her fingers as her excitement continued to mount. Nellie was panting now. Despite a slight breeze crossing the room, beads of perspiration formed on her forehead and cheeks and between her breasts. "We'll know soon enough," he said. "If things don't work out quite right between us, I'll still make sure you get out of Abilene without any harm coming to you from Hickok."

"I hope you're a man of your word," she gasped, jacking his cock harder, pulling the tip of it down until it touched the velvety soft hair of her mound. "I truly believe you are, or I wouldn't be here tonight . . . doing this. We only met a few hours ago. Whether you believe it or not, I'm not the kind of woman who makes promises she doesn't keep. I'll do whatever you say, only just please don't leave me here. Wild Bill will kill me."

He kept his doubts to himself, though it mattered little to him. Nellie was giving him pleasure, and he took it wherever he could find it when a woman was beautiful. "I never once thought you were that kind, Nellie. You're in a bad situation right now, but I also think we're attracted to each other. I can only speak for myself. I find I'm attracted to you, even if we did meet in the middle of a Kansas prairie."

"I'm very attracted to you," she said, inching her body closer to his, pressing the swollen end of his pulsating prick between the moist lips of her cunt.

"That feels good," he said, pushing his buttocks forward, adding pressure.

"Oh John, yes it does," she moaned, moving her head from side to side on the pillows, her eyelids tightly closed for the moment. "Lie between my legs. I want you desperately now. I can't wait much longer."

Nellie rolled over on her back, parting her milky thighs so he could enter her.

"That's an invitation I can't refuse," he told her, lifting his two-hundred pound body over her left leg and stomach, then lowering himself as gently as he could until he lay atop her, her warm breasts rubbing the swirls of his dark chest hair. He could feel the rapid beat of her heart.

She quickly found his cock again with her hand and guided it toward her honeypot, rubbing the tip up and down until the wet lips of her cunt opened for him.

He gave a soft grunt and pushed the end of his prick between slick folds of her hot flesh, and found that her cunt was tight, too tight for him to enter her until she gave him more room.

"It won't fit," she complained, her hands and body

shaking with desire. "I was afraid it was too big. Push just a little bit harder. You must try."

"Give it time, darlin'. There's no rush. It's gonna fit in a minute."

"But I can't wait. I want it *now*."

He did his best to oblige her, ramming his cock a tiny bit deeper inside her, until he felt too much pressure and ended his thrust.

"Oh! Oh! That hurts me . . . only it feels good at the same time."

He kissed her again and drew his lips away. "Relax. Enjoy the way it feels. In time, you'll open up for me and then it'll feel mighty good."

"I'm not sure it will go in, as much as I hope it will."

"It will. Open your legs a little more."

Nellie did as he instructed, widening the gap between her thighs as far as she could. He took both hands and cupped the backs of her knees, lifting her legs off the mattress until her feet were aimed toward the ceiling.

Then he added pressure on his cock again, tightening the muscles in his buttocks. Another half inch of his prick went slowly inside her cunt, until the entire tip was buried in its wet heat.

"Oh my!" she cried, louder than he wished she had, not wanting to attract any attention to what was going on in his room should someone happen to be passing by the hotel. She dug her fingernails into his back and pursed her lips to keep her mouth closed.

"There," he said hoarsely, feeling his balls begin to rise. "Now we're gettin' somewhere."

Very slowly at first, whimpering softly, Nellie began to hunch back and forth ever so slightly. Cords of muscle stood out in her neck. She clamped her teeth together, making small sounds, a mixture of pleasure and pain.

He felt the walls of her cunt relax, only a fraction, and this allowed him to push himself inside her a little more. A sudden gasp for air came from deep within her chest and she began to tremble from head to toe with enough vigor to cause the bed to quiver.

"Oh damn! Oh damn! I . . . never . . . felt . . . anything like this before." She said it breathlessly, yet she still rocked gently against the head of his cock, wanting more.

And Slocum found himself caught up in the same rising desire for her. Her womb was as hot as any he could recall and he could feel her wetness trickling down to his scrotum.

Nellie thrust harder, faster, clawing his back with her fingernails until he was certain she'd drawn blood.

With a suddenness that surprised him, the walls of her cunt released their fierce grip on the tip of his prick. He pushed his member slowly but steadily into her depths.

Her mouth flew open, but before she could let out a scream he placed his mouth over hers, smothering the sound. Her spine arched up off the mattress, then her cry faded away with a rush of hot breath.

"Oh John! I'm coming!" Nellie started to slam her mound against the thicker base of his shaft, straining every muscle in her body, digging her heels into the bedsheets.

He met her increasing thrusts with movements of his own, a wet, sucking sound coming from their coupling. She bit her lower lip to hold a cry in her throat and rose off the mattress on her shoulders and heels, shaking violently the moment her full release arrived.

"Oh my!" she hissed between gritted teeth.

Slocum felt his his rising while he continued to pound his organ deeper, harder, faster.

Nellie fell back on the bed under his weight and as a

result of the power of his thrusts. She sounded like she was choking as she tried to take in enough air.

His orgasm was there, seconds away, when Nellie began to hammer her groin against him again.

"More?" he whispered, mildly amused, for it had taken her but a moment to be ready to come again.

"Yes! Yes! Give me all of it, John!"

It was a request he couldn't comply with, for as he made an attempt to bury his prick all the way to the hilt, he found he was at the bottom of her well.

This did nothing to slow Nellie's drive toward ecstasy so soon after her first release. She dug her heels into his buttocks and pulled him deeper inside her with all her strength, a thin, high-pitched wail bubbling from her compressed lips in spite of her best efforts to silence it.

She came up off the mattress again, hoisting his full weight with the sheer strength of her orgasm. And at almost the same instant, Slocum's balls exploded inside her, spewing forth a hot stream of jism that forced his own quieter sounds of enjoyment and sheer pleasure from his throat.

Their thrusts slowed, then stopped altogether. They lay there, panting, allowing their wonderful sensations to dissipate at their own speed.

After the last of his seed leaked into her womb, he rose on his elbows and rolled off to one side, taking her in his arms. He was totally spent, unable to speak.

But Nellie found her voice as soon as she regained her breath. "Now, Mr. Slocum, will you take me with you out of Abilene?" she asked.

He gazed at her and grinned. "Darlin', I'd take you damn near anywhere you wanted to go."

She snuggled against him, resting her cheek on his shoulder. Then she said, "But what about Wild Bill?"

"You leave Marshal Hickok to me," he said.

"He can be a real ornery man when he's on the prod," she promised him.

He gazed at the ceiling a moment. "So can I, darlin.' You just ain't ever seen me on the prod."

"I'm still scared," she whispered a while later, holding him next to her.

"I've told you this before, Miss Nellie Cass. You leave the worryin' part to me . . ."

She let out a soft breath. "I don't reckon I'll be able to stop worryin' until I'm out of this town forever. Maybe when Wild Bill's a hundred miles behind me I'll be able to rest easier at night."

13

Hickok stormed into the rear of Maude's boardinghouse with fire in his eyes. It was almost eleven o'clock and he'd been drinking heavily.

Maude, a heavy, elderly woman with her gray hair tied up in a bun, glanced at him when he came in the kitchen. Maude was widely known across Abilene for taking no nonsense from tough cowboys or rowdiness from any source, if it took place inside her run-down boardinghouse in one of the worst sections of the Devil's Addition. All the regulars who inhabited the sin district knew Maude Sims carried a pistol inside her blouse and had on many occasions shown a willingness to use it when a customer got out of hand.

"What's got your feathers ruffled, Marshal?" she asked, continuing to peel the potatoes on her drainboard. She seemed unmoved by his obvious agitation.

"Where the hell's that whore?"

"What whore you talkin' about, Bill? I've got four who're boardin' with me now. You gotta be more helpful than that when you're inquiring about a woman who's for sale. Hell, I've got plenty of 'em stayin' with me, only I don't allow 'em to turn no tricks in one of my rooms. This is a boardin' house, not a damn whore-house."

"You know damn well which one I'm talkin' about, Maudie. Where's Nellie?"

Maude shrugged. "How the hell should I know? I know for a fact she ain't here now."

"I've done been told she's back in town with some big tall feller."

Maude nodded, hardly missing a stroke with her peeling knife as she replied. "They came an' left. He boarded his horse in my stable out back. The two of 'em left, only they didn't go at the same time. That was four or five hours ago, after Nellie took herself a sweet oil bubble bath an' put on her best dress, with her hair done up in a ribbon."

"Where were they headed?"

"Didn't say. It was easy to see she got all prettied up for him. Said she was gonna meet him some place for dinner 'round eight."

"Who the hell is this big gent, anyhow?"

"Told me his name was Slocum. John Slocum. Nellie said after he left that he was a bounty hunter of some kind, an' a railroad detective. I think she's real taken with him, only she didn't come right out an' say it."

"Nellie's *my* woman, Maude. Besides that, she owes me the eight dollars she gave you for back rent last week. I loaned her that damn money."

"She said this Mr. Slocum gave her the money she owed you, and she had enough for this week's room an' board left over from the handful she had. Now she paid in advance for a whole damn week."

"She did?" Hickok snapped, feeling the effects of too much wine wash through his brain.

"She swore to me she was gonna pay you back that

eight dollars she borrowed from you . . . said she'd do it tomorrow. I saw the money. All in silver. She'll pay you, Bill. Nellie ain't no bad girl . . . she's just been through some real hard times this year."

"I'm gonna hit her real hard across her lyin' mouth soon as I find her, the rotten little whore, runnin' out on me like she did."

Maude scowled. "I'd give that some real hard thinkin' if I was you, Marshal. This Slocum feller has the look about him. I got him figured for a mean son of a bitch. Not that you ain't a tough hombre yourself, Bill, only this Slocum could wind up bein' real hard to handle. He strikes me as the kind of feller who don't like to be pushed around."

"I ain't scared of no son of a bitch on this earth, Maudie, an' you oughta know it by now, after all these years here in Abilene."

"I wasn't sayin' you should be scared of him, Marshal. Just keep a sharp eye on him if you aim to challenge him over Nellie. I've seen a lot of tough bastards come an' go in this town. Some ain't nothin' but talk, but this Slocum looks dangerous as hell to me."

"I didn't come here for no goddamn advice, Maudie," he said, wheeling for the door. "Just wanted to know where the hell the little whore was."

"I figure she's with Slocum. She sure did get all prettied up for him."

Hickok banged out the rear screen door, fuming mad, ready to call out this bounty-hunting railroad detective if he found him with Nellie Cass tonight.

He was half stumbling across Texas Street for the Bull's Head when his deputy, Calvin Cobbs, hailed him from the darkness at the top of his voice. What Hickok needed more than any further conversation was a drink . . . maybe several of them, until his temper cooled.

Hickok halted when he recognized Cobbs's voice. "What the hell is it, Calvin? I'm on whorin' business an' I'm in somethin' of a hurry."

"I think I found the little whore you's lookin' for, Marshal. Nellie Cass. Am I right?"

"Where the hell did you see her?"

"Well sir, I didn't actually see her . . . not in the flesh, if you know what I mean."

"Then why the hell are you botherin' me when I've done told you I'm lookin' for her?"

"I think I know where she's at."

Hickok froze in his tracks, staring his young deputy hard in the eye. "Where the hell is that?"

"At the Drovers Inn."

Hickok made a face. "Hell, that little bitch is flat broke an' she owes me money. She can't afford to stay in no place like the Drovers."

Cobbs looked down at his boots a moment, resting the butt of his shotgun on the ground. "She ain't there by her lonesome, Marshal. She's with this feller—"

"That'll be this bounty hunter, goes by the name of John Slocum."

"Yessir, that's him. Only he ain't no ordinary bounty hunter by trade. I went back to the office an' looked up some old circulars we had from the Union Pacific an' the Kansas an' Pacific. He's an honest-to-goodness railroad detective with a badge an' all the legal federal authority he needs. He's also worked for Wells, Fargo, an' Company a few times. I found most of the old notices on him, the ones that didn't get throwed out when we cleaned up the office this spring. If it's the same man, he's an honest-to-goodness authorized railroad detective, an' a paid killer to boot."

"That don't make a damn bit of difference to me, Calvin. He's got my whore with him, just like he stole her from me, same as a piece of property."

Again, Calvin Cobbs had some difficulty looking Marshal Hickok in the eye. "He's a hired shootist, Marshal. When the big Cattlemans Bank got robbed down on the Texas border, he went over the Rio Grande an' killed half the sons of bitches the first day he was there. Brought the rest of 'em back to the Eagle Pass jail an' collected rewards on all of 'em. Did it single-handed, the bank notice said. Meaner'n a two-headed rattlesnake, an' on the way to Abilene he gunned down Bob Cole. I heard it myself from a drummer named Barnaby Watson. Cole wasn't no slouch with a pistol, if you'll remember, an' this Slocum feller gave Cole the first pull. He dared him to reach for his gun, accordin' to the drummer."

"Where did it happen?" Hickok asked.

"Down at Willow Creek. There was these cowhands who took your Nellie with him. Had her hands tied. Accordin' to the drummer, she sure as hell didn't want to be with 'em when Slocum rode up on 'em at the creek."

"Her hands were tied up?"

"That's what Mr. Watson said. This big Slocum feller, he ordered 'em to let her go or he'd kill all four of 'em. Two of them drovers knowed who Slocum was an' they throwed up their hands an' rode off."

Hickok rubbed his chin. "But Cole, he figured he might be a bit faster?"

"That's what the drummer said, only Slocum killed him before he could clear leather."

"So that's the fresh grave that young cowboy was talking about today. I sent him over to see Sheriff Butler to see if he could investigate. If it's outside the city limits, it's out of my jurisdiction. The cowhand said there was this fresh grave right next to the creek, and that the feller had a hole plumb through his heart."

Again, Calvin Cobbs seemed to have difficulty finding the right words to say. "If it was up to me, Marshal, I'd say that railroad detective done you a favor. He brought Miss Nellie back to Abilene after she'd been tied up an' hauled away from town against her will. An' he killed Bob Cole, the leader of the bunch who took her."

Still, Hickok's jaw turned to granite. "What Mr. Slocum don't understand yet is that Nellie is my woman. I need to find him so I can explain it to him."

"I figure he's stayin' at the Drovers."

"And you think Nellie's with him?"

"Can't say for sure, Marshal. I didn't see 'em go in there together with my own two eyes."

Hickok pulled one pistol, then the other, checking the loads before he holstered them again. "I think I'll go have a talk with this Mr. John Slocum right now."

"You want me to come along, Marshal?"

"Hell no!" Hickok spat. "I can handle my own damn affairs in this shithole town. This John Slocum, whoever the hell he is, he's just one man."

Calvin nodded. "Just wanted you to know ahead of time what sort of feller you'll be dealin' with, Wild Bill. This gent has a bad reputation for killin' folks."

"So do I, Deputy Cobbs. They didn't make me the City Marshal of Abilene because I know how to shoot stray dogs or collect city ordinance money."

"Sorry, sir. I was only offerin' to help . . . maybe back you up from the alley behind the Drover's."

"I don't need your goddamn help, Calvin. Now I'm gonna go across the street to the Bull's Head an' tell Ben Thompson I need a big mug of red wine to take with me."

"I sure wouldn't mind tailin' along, Marshal. Just to be on the safe side."

Hickok ignored Deputy Cobbs, storming across Texas Street to the Bull's Head.

When he pushed through the batwing doors, he saw Ben Thompson standing behind the bar. "Gimme a big mug of red wine, Ben," he said, strolling across the saloon floor in short, quick strides.

"What the hell's your hurry, Bill?" Thompson asked, reaching under the bar for a beer mug in order to pour the marshal a tall drink.

"I think I just found out where Nellie's stayin.' She's at the Drovers with the bounty hunter, John Slocum. Calvin just told me where to find 'em."

Ben poured Hickok's wine. "Just a word of advice, Bill," he said, returning the cork to the jug. "I talked to a U.S. Deputy Marshal who used to ride with Heck Thomas down in the Nations when they was havin' all that outlaw trouble."

"So?" Hickok asked, downing a thirsty swallow, then sleeving his lips dry.

"This feller's name was Bill Roberts . . . they call him Little Billy Roberts 'cause he's so damn short."

"Get to the point, Ben. What has Little Billy Roberts got to do with John Slocum?"

"Roberts knew all about Slocum. He said Marshal Heck Thomas had known him for years. He said this Slocum is one of the hardest men to kill he ever run across . . . that he don't back down from nobody, an' that he's as quick with a gun as any son of a bitch he ever saw. Tough with his fists, too."

"Are you tryin' to scare me off of him, Ben?"

"Nope," Thompson replied, wagging his head. "Just sayin' that it might get risky if you brace him."

"Well, that's damn sure what I'm gonna do if he's got my Nellie with him."

Thompson gave Hickok a lingering stare. "You gotta

ask yourself, Bill. Is one little cow town whore worth riskin' your life for? You've got three or four other whores you consort with all the time. How about going over to see Alice tonight an' wait till mornin' to look for Nellie? You said you liked Alice nearly best of all."

Hickok drank more wine, until his mug was empty. He was damn near too drunk to be at his best with a gun tonight. "I reckon I could go see Alice. I can always find that little bitch Nellie an' John Slocum tomorrow morning."

"Sounds like a better idea to me," Thompson said, refilling Hickok's glass. "Besides, Alice has got bigger tits than Nellie's. Anybody can see that."

Hickok nodded, taking the last free mug of wine. "I'll go hunt down Alice an' give her the ride of her life tonight. But if you see Nellie, you tell the little bitch I'm lookin' for her an' I want my damn money back . . . with interest."

14

Hickok pushed his way through the swinging doors into the Pink Garter, his mouth a thin line. A hush fell over the drinkers when they saw him. Almost every regular in the Devil's Addition knew about him and his surly moods when his belly was full of alcohol. He was as unpredictable as a Kansas twister after he got drunk.

"Where the hell's Alice?" he demanded, hands resting on the butts of his holstered pistols. His words were thick, the mark of a man who'd been drinking steadily.

"She's in . . . the back," a balding bartender said. "She's with some guy named Al. She won't be back there long, Marshal, I can promise you that."

"Tell her to get her ass out here." Hickok's tone left no doubts about his seriousness.

"But she's with a customer," the barman protested. "Hell, she won't be but another minute or two, Marshal. She's gotta make a livin'. This is a real bad time of year for cash customers, you know."

"I don't give a damn if she's with the president. Tell her to get her ass out here."

The bar owner, Dan Willis, wasn't quite willing to

111

give in yet. "I gotta make a livin' too, Bill. She's in one of them back rooms makin' me some room rent. I need the money this late in the year as bad as she does."

Hickok sauntered over to the bar. "Listen to me real good, Dan. You ain't got no gamblin' permit. You ain't got a permit to run whores. Your liquor license expired over a year ago, so don't tell me about how bad you need to make a goddamn livin' out of this place. I can close the Pink Garter down tonight if I take the notion. And I'm gonna take that notion unless Alice is out here in two minutes."

"But Bill—"

"I let you keep this place open because I'm a good-natured man, but my good nature's about to change unless you fetch Alice up front right now."

Willis lowered his face. "Okay, Bill, but it's sure as hell gonna be hard on business when word gets out that a randy cowboy can't finish the buck-jump he's paid for here at my establishment. Word like that sure spreads in a hurry up an' down them cow trails."

Hickok gave Dan a steely stare. "What'll be a helluva lot harder on business at the Pink Garter is for me to close it down for violation of city ordinances. That way, you won't have to worry 'bout what the drovers are saying about this place down in Texas."

"I understand, Bill. Just give me a minute to hurry 'em up. Hell, a cowboy who ain't seen a woman in three or four months don't take all that long to get his bronc rode, if you know what I mean."

"Just get the bitch out here," Hickok said. "Meantime, pour me a glass of red wine . . . a glass big enough to keep me occupied while you tell Alice an' Al to hurry. I ain't got all night. I got other business to attend to, unless I decide to shut this place down now."

"Sure thing, Bill." Willis brought out a big beer mug

and put it on the counter in front of Hickok. Then he placed a bottle of red wine beside it. "Now, you drink all of this you want, Marshal. It's on the house."

Other patrons of the Pink Garter, sensing trouble was in the making, left their tables quietly a few at a time and went out the batwing doors.

A piano player in a corner of the saloon stopped his music and went out a side door. Now, the place was silent enough to hear a pin drop.

Hickok poured a glass brimming with wine and gulped it down, still in a rage over Nellie. He didn't give a damn who this John Slocum was, or how good with a gun everyone said he was supposed to be. He'd shoot the son of a bitch and then beat some sense into Nellie's head.

A bleached-blonde woman in a faded green velvet gown came through a curtain leading to rooms at the back. Her hair was a mess and her lip paint was smeared all over her mouth. She made a feeble attempt at a smile when she saw Hickok. She had been pretty once, until the effects of opiates and whiskey and hard living had taken its toll on her.

She had pendulous breasts, filling the top of her gown, but with a noticeable sag to them now. There were dark circles under her pale green eyes, and she was drunk enough, or high enough on smoke from an opium pipe, to have a little bit of difficulty walking toward him.

"Howdy, Bill. What brings you?" Her voice was deep, husky from strong drink.

"You know damn well what brung me here."

"But I was with . . . a gentleman caller."

"You've never buck-jumped a gentleman in your life, Alice, if you don't count me."

Her smile faded. "That wasn't no nice thing to say to a lady, Bill."

"It's 'cause you goddamn sure ain't no lady, Alice Walker. You're a damn crib whore, an' I want you to earn your damn money with me tonight."

Alice frowned. "But I'd heard you'd taken up with that skinny little bitch, Nellie Cass."

"That was before. A man can change his mind."

Just then, a seriously drunken cowboy wearing a six-shooter came stumbling through the curtain behind Alice. He gave Hickok a bleary-eyed stare while he was fastening his pants and buckling on his gun belt.

"Just who the hell do you think you are, mister?" the cowboy asked. "I'd done paid for a quarter hour with Alice, an' we ain't been back there five minutes."

"Mind your own business and get the hell out of here, whoever the hell you are."

"Name's Al Jennings, an' don't no son of a bitch talk that way to me." He tried to focus on Hickok through slitted eyelids covering bloodshot eyeballs.

"Is that so?" Hickok replied coldly.

"Goddamn right it's so, you bastard. I'm Al Jennings. In case you ain't never heard of me afore. I ain't nobody's damn pushover. I spent my hard-earned money with this here woman, an' by God, I intend to get my money's worth. I know damn well you heard of Al Jennings from down in Fort Worth, Texas, before tonight."

"I have a feeling it'll be the last time I ever hear your name unless you shut the fuck up and clear out of this place right now."

Al stiffened. "I can see you're wearin' iron. Let's settle this like men. Reach for them goddamn smoke wagons, mister, an' I'll blow you plumb to eternity."

"Don't do it, Al," Alice pleaded. "This is City Marshal Wild Bill Hickok."

"I don't give a shit who the sumbitch claims to be," Al growled. "Bill Hickok is a scout for the army. All he ever done was massacre a bunch of Injuns for General Crook. This long-haired bastard damn sure ain't Wild Bill Hickok. He's dressed up like a goddamn city slicker."

"You could be makin' a real serious mistake, Al," Dan Willis said from behind the curtain. "The man across the bar is none other than Wild Bill Hickok. If I was you I'd shut my mouth an' get the hell out of here, if you aim to live long enough to see Fort Worth again."

Al's face twisted. "Don't no son of a bitch run me out of no saloon, don't make a damn who he is. And ain't no son of a bitch gonna take no paid whore away from me neither. Go fer your goddamn gun, you bastard. You look like a piece of yellow dog shit to me."

"Are you quite certain you're ready to die over a two-dollar whore, Mr. Jennings?" Hickok asked in a soft, even voice, with his mind already made up to kill the drover for nothing more than what he'd just said.

"Alice ain't no two-dollar whore," Al replied with heat in it. "I give her three whole dollars, only a sumbitch like you comes along so I can't get my money's worth. I ain't gonna stand for it."

"Enough talk," Hickok said. "You're heeled, same as I am. Fill your fist with iron whenever you think you're ready to be measured for a coffin."

Al's fingers curled near the walnut grips of his Navy Colt .44. "You're one dead son of a bitch, mister. They'll be fittin' you for a coffin before the sun comes up. I say you ain't nothin' but hot wind."

Having said that, Al's right hand dipped for his gun, a clumsy attempt at a fast draw made by a man too drunk to know the difference.

It would have been an easy shot against a drunk for

Hickok, using either hand. He chose to draw left-handed, simply as a way to polish his skills.

A forty-four caliber slug thundered inside the Pink Garter, filling the smoky room with noise.

Al Jennings was lifted off his feet by a bullet shattering his breastbone. He was slammed against the wall behind the bar, as blood sprayed all over the mirrors and clean glasses on Dan Willis's back shelves.

Jennings sank to the floor on his rump, blood pumping from his mouth when he tried to speak. All he could manage was a weak groan.

Alice let out a scream, backing away from the grisly sight as Dan Willis disappeared into the rear storage room while a wisp of blue gun smoke circled lazily toward the ceiling, smelling of burnt cordite.

Pink foam came from Al Jennings's mouth, along with a soft, bubbling, strangling sound.

"Bullet went through a lung," Hickok said, holstering his Colt. "Too bad. I was kinda interested in what he had to say now."

Jennings fell over on his side, one booted foot twitching with death throes. His pistol lay on the blood-soaked floor beside him.

Seconds later, when Willis was sure Al Jennings was dead, he came back into the front room.

Hickok gave the barman a grim smile. "Both of you saw it and I'll expect you to testify at the inquest. Mr. Al Jennings went for his gun first."

"No doubt about it," Willis stammered. "You shot him in self-defense."

"That's the God's truth," Alice whimpered. "He was all set to gun you down, Bill. You didn't have no choice but to shoot him before he shot you. I'll swear to it in court if that's what you want."

"Won't hardly any jury take the word of a whore

about any damn thing. Dan, you'll be the one to tell the judge how it happened."

"I sure will, Marshal. You can count on it."

"Enough of this talk," Hickok said, motioning to Alice. "I want you with me tonight. Get your ass out here an' we'll head over to my place."

He had a final thought, looking across the empty barroom at Dan Willis. "If Deputy Cobbs shows up, you tell him exactly how it happened, and that I'll fill out the necessary paperwork in the morning. Meantime, if I was you, I'd get a mop and start cleaning up all that blood. Send for old man Woodson, the undertaker, so he can haul the body off before it starts to stink in this heat."

"I'll send for Mr. Woodson right away, Marshal," Willis promised, as Hickok led Alice out of the Pink Garter into the dark of night.

As soon as they were away from the lights from the windows of the Pink Garter, Hickok grabbed Alice's arm in a fierce grip and slapped her hard across the face.

Alice tumbled to the boardwalk, covering a bleeding lower lip with her hand. "Why'd you go an' do that, Bill? I came as soon as Dan told me you was askin' for me."

"You took too damn long getting there. Next time I send for you, I want you to come a-running."

She struggled to her feet, having some difficulty in high-heel shoes. "Sorry, Bill," she mumbled, running the tip of her tongue across her swollen lip. "Dan didn't tell me you was in such a hurry."

He glared at her. "When I ask for you, bitch, I'm always in a hurry."

"I said I was sorry."

"Start walking toward my place," he demanded.

"I gotta take off these shoes first, Bill, or I'm liable to fall down."

The darkness kept too many others from seeing them and the sin district was quiet when he replied, "I'm liable to knock you down again unless you start walking toward my place. Now get moving!"

Alice stumbled off the boardwalk, trying to keep her balance in dry wagon ruts as Hickok walked behind her, feeling better about things. He'd just killed a man . . . in self-defense, even if he had goaded him into it to a degree.

"It feels good to kill a man who needs killin'," he told Alice. "Makes your blood rush a little."

15

T. C. Henry, accompanied by Deputy City Marshal Cobbs, came bursting through the doors of the Pink Garter at three o'clock in the morning.

Woodrow Woodson, the city undertaker, along with two youthful assistants, were seeing to the removal of the late Al Jennings into a dusty black hearse drawn by two black horses parked in front of the saloon.

It was late, and most of the Devil's Addition was quiet now as its few customers went to bed.

The coppery smell of blood filled the drinking establishment when T. C. Henry walked in, permeating stale air already heavy with tobacco smoke and the scent of warm beer, the stench of unwashed spittoons.

"What happened here?" Henry asked Dan Willis the moment he stepped inside. Henry was wearing a long nightshirt stuffed into the tops of his pants. A bowler hat was pushed back on his head. A small caliber pistol showed above the waistband of his tweed trousers. Beads of sweat had formed on his brow, due to his haste to reach the Pink Garter after Deputy Cobbs awakened him to inform him of the shooting incident.

"Marshal Hickok shot one of my payin' customers," Willis replied. "Killed him, Mr. Henry, an' all he was doin' was rentin' a bed an' spendin' some time with one of the gals, Alice Walker."

"How did it happen?" Henry inquired, glancing around the lamplit room.

"I gotta be real careful what I say, Mr. Henry, you bein' the Chairman of the Dickenson County Protective Association an' all. I don't need no legal troubles. An' I sure as hell don't want no difficulties with Marshal Hickok. He can make it mighty rough on a businessman here if he takes the notion, an' he's liable to on account of Alice."

"Why would you fear legal troubles from our appointed city marshal, Mr. Willis?"

"If he takes the inclination, he can put an honest businessman out of business in the city of Abilene. In case you ain't heard, he's done it plenty of times before if somebody happens to cross him"

Henry stepped over to the bar, then he motioned for Deputy Cobbs to step outside as two of the undertaker's assistants took the corpse through the swinging doors outside to load it in the hearse.

"You can tell me what happened in the strictest confidence, Mr. Willis."

Willis seemed uncertain at first, glancing around to be sure the saloon was empty.

"Spreak freely, Mr. Willis," Henry urged. "I need to know the details of the matter."

"There was this cowboy up from Texas. Name was Al Jennings. He was in one of my back rooms with Alice . . . if you get my meaning here. I don't want you to think I'm doin' anything illegal. All I do is rent rooms. I don't ask a helluva lot of questions about what goes on in 'em when I rent some trail hand one of my beds for a spell."

"I understand. He was paying for time with a prostitute, so please continue. I'm not so naive that I don't know what goes on in this part of town."

"Marshal Hickok walks in," Dan continued. "It was easy to see he'd been drinkin' a lot. He gets kinda pushy when he's had a few too many."

"Nothing new about that. Then what happened?" Henry's brow furrowed.

"Hickok demanded that I go get Alice out of Al Jennings's room afore they was . . . done with their business. Jennings had done paid for her, I reckon, an' paid me for the room so I didn't ask no questions. Wasn't none of my affair what the two of them done back there."

"What happened then?" Henry still seemed unable to put all the pieces together.

"I asked Wild Bill to wait, that Alice wouldn't be but a few more minutes."

"What did Hickok say?"

"He ordered me to go fetch her right then an' there. He said he wanted to see her now."

"He couldn't wait a few minutes . . . long enough for Alice's . . . business transaction to be completed?"

"Nope. Then he said that if I wouldn't do it, he'd close me down for good an' I'd be out of business inside the city limits of Abilene, which fell under his jurisdiction. He made that part real plain."

"On what grounds?" Henry asked.

Dan looked askance a moment. "I'm a little bit behind on my permit fees. Not much, mind you, but just a month or two, since business has been so bad after most of the drovers up from Texas went back home."

"But what about the shooting? Let's cut through the

other stuff and tell me how this Jennings fellow got shot.
You haven't told me what I need to know." Henry's tone
had risen an octave or two, revealing his impatience with
the discussion they were having.

"Hickok made me bring Alice out front, right here
where all them bloodstains are. He told her she had to
go with him right then."

"Where was Mr. Jennings?" Henry asked.

"Still in the back room puttin' on his clothes, I reckon.
I didn't go back to have a look."

"Then how did the killing occur? If Mr. Jennings was
in the back room, and Marshal Hickok and this Alice
woman were here in the saloon, how did the shooting
happen?"

"Al was a little on the drunk side, an' he was mad-
der'n hell when I told Alice she had to come up front
right away or there'd be serious trouble."

Henry nodded. "I take it that not long afterward, Mr.
Jennings showed up here in the saloon."

"Yessir, he did. Came through that curtain yonder,
right behind me."

"Did Jennings have a gun?"

"He was bucklin' it on when he came in here," Dan
said, "but I figured he'd be smart enough to keep his
mouth shut in front of Wild Bill Hickok, him bein' the
city marshal, not to mention his bad reputation for killin'
folks all these years. Hell, I had it judged that Al would
keep his mouth shut an' go outside, or damn near anyplace else. I never dreamed he'd get smart with Wild
Bill over a whore."

"I'm sure Jennings was peeved."

Dan scowled. "I ain't sure exactly what that means,
but he was damn sure pissed off on account of he didn't
get all his time with Alice."

"Time he'd already paid for," Henry said, knowing it

had to be the fuse that lit the powder keg between Bill Hickok and Al Jennings.

"That's right. He paid for a quarter of an hour with Alice an' he paid me for the room. Cash money. He was entitled to the time with her, an' for the room."

Henry let out a sigh. "Marshal Hickok may have gone too far this time. The town council may not take this tragic event lightly, when the facts are made known to the men who govern this city."

"Hickok was real smart about it," Dan said softly, making sure no one outside could hear him.

"How's that?"

"Hickok knew Jennings was drunk, that he wasn't no match for him in a gunfight."

"Then how did it happen? Why did the marshal let things go so far?"

"Can't nobody figure the way Wild Bill thinks when he's bad drunk."

"What did Hickok say?" Henry wanted to know, pursing his lips.

"He told Jennings he was takin' Alice with him right then, an' if Al didn't like it, he could go for his gun any damn time he pleased."

"In other words, Marshal Hickok goaded a drunken cowboy into pulling a gun on him."

Dan nodded. "That way, it would be self-defense, an' me an' Alice would have to testify to it in court. Bill knew he had us as witnesses."

Henry turned away from the bar as the hearse pulled away from the Pink Garter. "Marshal Hickok may have pushed his luck a bit too much tonight. This event may have cost Bill Hickok his job."

"Like I said, Mr. Henry, I'll have to testify before the judge that it was self-defense. Jennings went for his gun first, an' Hickok killed him. That's the way it actually happened, only Al was too drunk to know what he was doin', an' Marshal Hickok was just drunk enough to be lookin' for a gunfight he was sure he could win. Now, I ain't gonna say all that in front of no judge or jury, but that's the truth about how it all come about tonight."

Henry's shoulders slumped in apparent resignation. "Our city marshal has gotten away with this sort of thing far too many times in the past. A thing like this could ruin a town's reputation among visiting cattlemen. We could wind up with a ghost town on our hands if the cow herds head for Dodge City or down to Hays, or Newton. In case you've forgotten, Hickok killed one of his own deputies last year over some minor disturbance having to do with a dog. Word like that spreads in a hurry."

Dan almost whispered when he said, "Somethin's gotta be done about it, Mr. Henry. I'm hearin' more an' more complaints about Wild Bill all the time. He gets drunk damn near every night, an' he spends more time consortin' with the ladies an' drinkin' wine than he does enforcin' the law. I've been hearin' a lot more of it lately."

"So have I," Henry replied. "It seems the marshal's drinking problem may have gotten completely out of hand at times. I am afraid something will have to be done about it. This incident will force me to bring the marshal's behavior before the town council."

"Don't get me wrong," Dan continued. "We need a tough city marshal to handle some of them rowdy drunks when the herds come in. Hell, I've got so damn many bullet holes in my ceiling that when it rains, I don't even have to mop the floors. Most of the blood an' tobacco stains wash right out the front doors."

"How well I know," Henry said. "Ben Thompson's Bull's Head leaks like a sieve in the winter when it does rain. But if Ben Thompson won't complain about it, there isn't much the town council can do. Ben Thompson and Hickok have been friends for years. I understand Ben gets special treatment from our city marshal when it comes to gambling permits and a number of other things."

Dan glanced down at the bloodstains on his floor, then the bullet holes in his roof. "Most of us in the district have learned to keep our mouths shut, Mr. Henry. If we say anything about our troubles, Wild Bill comes down hard on us an' he's shut down more'n a few places when the owners didn't cooperate with him.

"Someone has to bring an end to this lawlessness. And the sad part of it is, our biggest problems are with the duly sworn lawmen we have here. Most of them, anyway. County Sheriff Roy Butler quickly learned to look the other way when certain violations of the law were going on. He rarely ever arrests anyone for even the most serious infraction.

"All I'm tryin' to do here is make a livin', Mr. Henry. I ain't lookin' to cause no trouble."

"Where is Marshal Hickok now?"

"He's with Alice."

"I'm sure he took her to his quarters behind the jail. A fine state of affairs, when our chief city peace officer kills a man so he can take a prostitute to his sleeping room that the city provides for him."

Dan put on his apron and carried a mop bucket and mop to the bloodstained floor. "I've got no idea where he took her, Mr. Henry."

"I think you know where he took her, only you're afraid to say it publicly."

Willis began mopping the dried blood with pine cleaner, as if he had no more to say. But after a few strokes, he looked up at Henry. "You gotta understand my position, Mr. Henry. I'm gonna testify that Bill Hickok killed Al Jennings in self-defense, which is mostly the truth. That's all I'm gonna say if the judge asks me."

"I understand, Mr. Willis," Henry replied. "But please tell me one more thing ... in confidence, of course. What brought on this violent incident? Something must have set Marshal Hickok off tonight."

"That's easy. A little bitty whore named Nellie. She left town with four cowboys. Run out on him, owin' him eight dollars. Then she came back with this tall stranger who goes by the name of John Slocum. He's a bounty hunter, or so they say, and a railroad detective."

Henry strolled to the front doors of the Pink Garter. "I suspect it won't be long before this John Slocum becomes Hickok's next victim."

Dan continued to mop his floor. "From what I hear about Slocum, I wouldn't be too sure about that ..."

16

His dreams were fitful things, a kaleidoscope of events from his distant past as a boy growing up in Calhoun County, Georgia, in the Allegheny Mountains. Drifting off to sleep after another moment of ecstasy with Nellie, when she told him she and her family came west from Georgia, he recalled how he was a Georgian by birth and this simple reminder of Slocum's often troubled yet happy youth put his thoughts back to those times, he supposed, although he wondered how Nellie had been able to bring his past back so clearly when so many years, difficult years, had passed since then.

In his dreams, Slocum recalled his father vividly, a strong man with stronger principles who came home from the war with a minnie ball buried inside him. William Slocum, wound-weakened, succumbed to a wasting disease and soon thereafter, went to his grave.

His mother, Opal grieved endlessly over the death of her husband. Less than a year thereafter, she followed William to a burial plot, beside him under a towering oak tree behind the log house on their family farm.

And his beloved older brother, Robert, had been killed

at Gettysburg while serving as a lieutenant with Pickett's Division at Little Round Top, one of the bloodiest conflicts of the war. John returned home to Calhoun County, burdened by his brother's death, only to discover he was alone, without a suviving member of his family to welcome him.

He was filled with bittersweet memories, of his father and his gentle mother's delicious meals, her tenderness, the love she gave her sons. And of growing up with Robert, all the mischief they got in, the many fights they all too often had backing each other at school or at a Saturday night dance. Most of the bare-knuckled contests had been over girls, for pretty women were also a driving force in Robert's life. Both brothers began their attempts at courtship of the region's most beautiful maidens at the age of thirteen. Robert was a better horseman, but when it came to getting under a youthful girl's skirt, John and his dark green eyes, accompanied by a gift for saying the right words at the most opportune time, far outdistanced his brother in the game of seduction.

Their hard work, laboring alongside their father in the fertile fields of their holdings, breaking ground with a team of mules behind a walking cultivator, cutting and splitting firewood and other chores around a farm, had turned them into strong men early in life. After work, he and Robert explored every nook and valley across the Alleghenys surrounding their farmland and by the time they were in their teens, they knew every bear wallow and cave, every high mountaintop, the creeks and swimming holes, becoming excellent woodsmen and hunters. Slocum and his brother kept their larder full of venison and all manner of wild game, for they both demonstrated an early knack for hunting and marksmanship.

Those had been wonderful times. Until they ended so

suddenly with the secessionist move to form the Confederacy, a call to arms every Slocum was ready to answer with Brown Bess muskets and pistols, laying their lives on the line for a cause even though William Slocum never owned slaves. It was an experience that would change John Slocum's life forever, ofttimes robbing him of sleep when unwanted dreams of bloody battles returned to haunt him again and again.

When he came back from the brutal war, finding nothing but empty buildings and land gone to seed, his father and mother buried behind the barn, he went through an even deeper internal change. Bitter, angry at men who drew his loved ones into a conflict that took them away from him, a final dark event came his way.

Yankees occupied Georgia and the South. Reconstructionist judges, sometimes called carpetbaggers, ruled the defeated Southern states, bleeding what was left of the South's assets into their own pockets.

A Reconstruction judge with jurisdiction over Calhoun County drove out to the Slocum farm one day, not long after he got home to mourn his losses.

The judge brought along a hired gunman in his carriage, an enforcer to carry out his public and private orders. The judge allowed as how he now owned the Slocum place, and insisted he bought it for back taxes due while the men of the family were away at war. The place was now his.

Slocum protested angrily. His family's farm was one thing he vowed the Yankees would never take from him. This did nothing to stop the judge from ordering him off the land by the end of the week, or he would be forcibly removed at gunpoint and then taken to jail for trespass.

Slocum declared that any man who thought he was capable of carrying out such an unjust eviction was welcome to try it at any time he felt he was ready.

The judge's gunslick reached for his pistol.

John Slocum's war experiences had turned him into a man skilled with most any weapon. He drew his Navy Colt and shot the gunman through his heart, and when the overfed judge reached inside his suit coat to draw a hidden firearm, Slocum put a bullet squarely between his eyes.

With two dead men to account for, one being a powerful judge with absolute authority over Calhoun County in the aftermath of the war, Slocum knew he could never get a fair trial anywhere in Georgia from another Reconstruction judge presiding over his case, for a Yankee judge would sentence a judge-killer to the maximum penalty, a certain death at the end of a hangman's rope after a carefully handpicked Union sympathizer jury found him guilty of two murders, for there were no witnesses to the shootings.

Left with no choices, soon to be a wanted man with a reward out on his head, Slocum made the only choice he could.

Sadly, fighting back old memories of happier times, he set fire to the house, barns, and springhouse, burning the William Slocum farm to the ground.

Saddling one of two starving horses he'd been allowed to keep under the terms of Lee's surrender, armed with his pistol and a Spencer carbine he took off a dead Yankee, he rode away from the smoldering ruins where he'd grown up, never to return. He did not look back when he crested a hill riding a dirt lane away from his former home.

Heading west, where he knew the frontier was populated by countless men on the run from the law, he made his way across what was left of the war-torn South to begin a new life, and to leave his beginnings behind.

• • •

That had been many years ago, and by now the warrant for his arrest was long forgotten, however he had no desire to see that farm again. It was a part of his happier past and he wanted to forget the memories visiting the land would evoke. There was no going back to those times. All his family members were gone now and there was nothing he could do to bring them back.

A shaft of gray dawn finally awakened him from this strange dream. He rubbed his eyelids open and glanced around the room. Nellie lay there beside him, curled into a ball, her lovely yellow hair spread across one cheek.

He thought about her a moment. She wasn't the keeping kind of woman and he wasn't looking for a "keeper". Until his urges to see what was on the other side of the next mountain or hill finally left him, he was destined to live a solitary life.

But when a beautiful young woman like Nellie came along, offering him her womanly charms, he would enjoy them for a while. It had been this way for years, ever since the war was over, and nothing in his immediate future held any promise of bringing about a change.

He was still searching for something, although he had no idea what, or who, it might be. When the need to move on struck him, he rarely hesitated saddling his horse and striking off in any direction he chose. A free life was what he wanted for himself, and Slocum intended to keep it that way.

He sat up in bed, recalling his brief encounter with Bob Cole, a heated exchange of words before Slocum had no choice but to shoot him down.

I wonder if his friends try me, he thought, if I put

Nellie on a horse I'll buy for her this morning to carry her away from Abilene.

Or would Marshal Wild Bill Hickok try his hand at stopping Slocum from taking her away, since according to Nellie, she was Wild Bill's woman?

Swinging his legs off the mattress, the motions he made gave Nellie a start.

Her eyes flew open. She blinked furiously for a few moments as if she couldn't quite get her bearings or figure out where she was. Then she saw Slocum and smiled, reaching for his hand. "I thought I was in Bill's room and he was coming back to knock me around the way he did so many times before. He thinks he owns me."

"That ain't gonna happen," he said, squeezing her palm to reassure her. "How many times do I have to tell you that you're safe now?"

"I like to hear it, after all he's put me through. I think I'm afraid to believe it's really gonna happen, that I'll be free of him."

Slocum got up, stretching trail-weary muscles before he started to dress, pulling on his denims and boots before fixing his money belt around his waist. "I'm goin' over to the livery stable now to inquire about buyin' you a gentle horse and a saddle. Lock the door behind me and don't let anybody in. I'll take the key with me."

Nellie climbed out of bed, wonderfully naked, her breasts swaying gently on her rib cage. She put her arms around him as he was stepping into his pants. "I'll be scared the whole time you're gone, John. Please don't let anything happen to you. I don't think you understand. Bill can be real mean. He gets the chance, he'll gun you down from behind."

He took her arms from his neck and slipped into his blue shirt. "I won't give him that chance, so stop your worryin'. Get dressed. We're pullin' out of Abilene as soon as I talk to the sheriff, to tell him what happened between me and Bob Cole down at Willow Creek, and then I'll get you a horse and saddle. I won't be gone very long."

She kissed him on the cheek and went over to her valise to find something to wear. Slocum strapped on his gun belt and dust-covered gray Stetson hat, its crown turned dark by sweat stains. He tugged the front of the hat's flat brim down low over his eyes. "Remember what I said, Nellie. Lock this door and don't open it for any reason till I get back. I'll conduct my business with the county sheriff and the local liveryman as quickly as I can."

He walked to the door, twisting the inside latch with the room key in his pocket. He checked the hall both ways, then the stairway.

At this early hour, only a few of Abilene's citizens were out and about in the early gray of dawn. Slocum's belly felt empty and he made up his mind to get something to eat at the first opportunity, bringing something back to the room for Nellie after his visit with Sheriff Butler and the stable owner was out of the way.

"Good-bye, John," Nellie said, smiling.

"*Adios*, pretty lady," he replied, closing the door behind him.

He heard the door latch click as he strolled into the hall to walk downstairs. Everyone staying at the Drover's Inn appeared to be sound asleep.

Walking out on the front porch of the hotel, his nose scented coffee and fatback being cooked. "Damn I'm hungry," he muttered, his belly growling, although he continued toward the center of town, where he expected to find Sheriff Butler's office close to the town square.

"Buenas dias, señor," an elderly woman said to him as he passed her on the road.

"Buenas dias a ti," he replied, wishing her the same good morning in Spanish, finding it odd that a woman of Mexican blood would be in Abilene.

Slocum was totally unprepared for what he heard next, the piercing sound of a woman's scream behind him. Instinctively he whirled around, jerking his Colt free of its holster.

"Que pasa?" he asked her.

The old woman pointed to a spot on the ground near a boardwalk.

"What is it?" he asked her again, this time in English when he saw nothing that should have caused her so much alarm, for the road was empty.

"Mirra, señor!" she exclaimed.

He gave the dry, rutted roadway a closer inspection with his gun fisted. Then he saw what had frightened the old woman.

A rattlesnake was slithering toward the boardwalk, a four-foot diamondback.

Slocum chuckled and holstered his Colt. "Do not worry, *señora*. The snake will not harm you if you leave it alone. It is only like me . . . looking for something to eat."

The woman smiled and walked a wide circle around the snake before it disappeared underneath the boardwalk.

17

Alice cringed against a back wall of the room, blood trickling from a corner of her mouth, her dress torn down the front so that the milky tops of her breasts were exposed. Skies outside the lone window of the city marshal's office were graying with dawn. Somewhere in another part of the city, a cock crowed to announce the arrival of sunrise.

"Get that dress off, bitch!" Hickok snarled. "I want to see you plumb naked, like you were for that shithead cowboy I had to kill, on account of you."

"Sure thing, Bill. Only please don't hit me again," Alice croaked, cowering on the floor on her hands and knees after the beating Bill had given her. "I'll do anything you say, only I'm beggin' you not to hit me no more. I ain't done nothin' to deserve havin' you hit me so hard. How come you're so mad at me?"

"I'm gonna bust your skull unless you do what I tell you to do." He tipped back the last of a bottle of wine, leaning against the wall of his sleeping quarters behind the Abilene city jail, blocking the door so Alice could not escape. "You deserve a good ass-whippin' because you didn't come out when I sent Dan back to fetch you. When I send for you, I expect you come to me right then."

"I'll do anything you want, Bill, only don't hurt me no more. Please. I was with Al, an' he'd already paid me his money. You ain't asked for me in months . . . not since early in the spring."

"Get that dress off. It don't make a damn when I ask for you. You come when I send for you. I'm tired of listenin' to your shit, you rotten whore. Now get them goddamn clothes off before I have to slap you again."

Alice straightened up and pulled the shoulder straps down on her gown until the garment slid to the floor in a pool of torn velvet around her slender ankles. She was trembling with fear when she looked up at Bill.

"That's better," Hickok said, draining the bottle of French red in his fist.

Alice stood there in her corset and stockings. "How come you had to kill that cowboy, Bill? He was drunk. He wasn't no match for you. All he was doin' was payin' me for my time. He didn't deserve to die. Didn't seem like there was no need for you to kill him. He didn't deserve to die like that, not with him bein' drunk like he was."

"He went for his gun, you stupid whore. Deserving has got nothing to do with it. We're all gonna die some-time, only he got his a few years early. If the son of a bitch had kept his mouth shut and gone on about his business, he'd still be alive to pay you for another night."

"But you pushed him into it. He was harmless as a fly, an' you killed him," Alice whimpered. "He wasn't nothin' but a trail hand, a drover up from Texas who didn't know nothin' about you or how bad you are to use a gun."

"Shut the fuck up an' take that corset off. He was dumb enough to reach for his gun. A trail hand with any sense won't reach for no gun against me. There's bodies layin' out on Boot Hill to prove it. Lots of 'em, and Al Jennings is gonna go to the big sleep with the others. I can kill any son of a bitch in Kansas who comes at me with a pistol. Al Jennings was dumb as a rock to draw on me."

"Sure, Bill, I know you're good with a gun, only don't get mad at me. All I was doin' was askin' how come you went an' killed him."

"I already explained it. He made a move to draw his pistol. I shot him in self-defense."

"Okay, Bill, okay." Alice began unfastening her corset strings, slowly releasing the ample body she had tucked inside her tight undergarment.

"You're gettin' old, Alice," Hickok said casually. "Your tits are damn near hangin' down to your knee-caps, and your face looks like shit, all wrinkled up like it was burnt in some kind of fire."

"Jesus, Bill. I don't look *that* bad, do I?"

"You do right now. Get that goddamn corset off, an' then lay down on the bed."

"Anything you want, Bill. I ain't never refused to do anything you asked me to do, have I?"

He pushed away from the wall, his eyes glued to Alice's sagging breasts. "You didn't come out of that goddamn room at the Pink Lady when I wanted."

"But I had a . . . customer. He'd already paid me for the time."

"That don't mean a damn thing when I tell you I need you right then. It don't make a shit who you're with, or how much he's paid you."

"But—"

"I can lock you up in a jail cell out front. Prostitution

is against the law in Abilene. I can have Judge Green give you up to thirty days. I can have you run plumb out of this town if I want."

Alice stepped out of her stockings. "You never done nothin' like that to Nellie. What makes Nellie Cass so damn special that make you wanna treat me this way?"

"Shut up about Nellie!"

"All I was was sayin' was—"

"I said shut the fuck up about Nellie. I ain't in the mood to talk about her nohow."

"I heard she left town last week, headed for Texas with four drovers."

"She's back," Hickok said, his voice turning huskier when he stared at Alice's naked body. "But that ain't none of your affair, bitch, so don't mention her name to me again or I'll have to hurt you."

"Please don't hit me no more, Bill. I'll do whatever you want me to do. I swear. You know I've always done my best to please you."

"Lie down on that bed. Spread them legs apart so I can get between 'em."

"Sure thing, Bill," Alice replied, stumbling over to a cot sitting against the west wall, where a thick mattress with dirty sheets and a pair of goose down pillows propped against the headboard made up Hickok's bed. She wiped the blood from her lips again before she sat on the edge of the mattress.

She lay down as he wanted her to, opening her thighs so the swirls of hair around her mound were exposed in the light from an oil lamp beside the bed.

"I'm gonna fuck you real hard," Hickok said, pulling off his buckskin shirt, then unfastening his gun belt, and his pants.

"You know I like it hard, Bill. I like it when you fuck me real hard."

"It's gonna be harder than usual, you lousy rotten whore."

"Why's that, Bill? An' why are you callin' me all them names when I said I'd do whatever you wanted?"

"On account of that damn drunk cowboy you forced me to kill at the Pink Garter. If you'd have kept your damn mouth shut an' come out front when I told Dan Willis I wanted you, that son of a bitch would still be alive."

"He was drunk, Bill. An' he'd already paid his money for me an' the room. I already told you that . . . why I couldn't come out right then."

"I don't give a damm about any of that, bitch. When I send for you, I want you to come runnin'," he said, jutting his jaw as he pulled the cork on another bottle of red French wine Dan Willis had given him.

"I was tryin' to come out quick, only Al was raising a big ruckus on account of he'd paid me his money an' he'd paid for the room."

Hickok grinned mirthlessly as he shucked down his pants to pull off his boots. "The dumb son of a bitch ain't raisin' no ruckus now. He's dead, in case you didn't notice. I killed him with one shot. I'm liable to do the same thing to you, bitch, if you don't fuck me real good right now. I can do damn near anything I want in this town. I'm the city marshal, just in case you forgot."

Alice drew back on the bed, her eyes round with fear as Hickok dropped his clothes on the floor.

The bedsprings squeaked. Hickok rammed his cock into her cunt with as much force as he could muster, holding her head by two fistfuls of hair. The cast-iron headboard banged against the wall with each thrust he made, somehow adding to his pleasure for the moment.

"Fuck me harder, Bill," Alice groaned. "Fuck me so hard that it hurts."

"I *am* fucking you hard, slut," he replied, his teeth clenched. "You've fucked so goddamn many cowboys that can't no man do you any good."

"That . . . ain't . . . so," Alice gasped, wrapping her fingers around the iron rods of the headboard as Hickok's thrusts became faster. "I been . . . savin' myself . . . for you, Bill, only . . . you had your fancies set . . . on Nellie."

His hunching stopped abruptly. He raised himself up on one elbow and swung a powerful backhand across Alice's cheek, twisting her head on the pillows.

Tears flooded her eyes. "Why did you go an' do that to me, Bill?" she cried.

"I already told you not to talk about Nellie no more! You don't hear too good!"

"I'm sorry, Bill."

"Saying you're sorry ain't good enough."

"What else can I do?"

He pulled his limp prick out of her cunt, rolling over on his side to grab the fresh bottle of wine. "You can suck me," he said gruffly.

A silence. Hickok pulled thirstily on the bottle of French red. "Did you hear me, whore?" he asked.

"You . . . know I don't do that. Sucking on a man's pecker is for cheap women who can't do no better."

"You're saying you ain't cheap?"

"Hell, no, I ain't cheap."

"Then how come you was with Al Jennings tonight, for two lousy dollars?"

"It was three, Bill."

"Three?"

"A dollar was for the room an' two shots of his sour mash whiskey."

Hickok drank wine again. "Forget it, Alice. I ain't interested in you."

She sat up in bed. "It's because Nellie's back in town, ain't it?"

"That ain't none of your affair. I just ain't interested in poking you now."

She saw his cock go limp between his legs. "You've only got eyes for her, ain't you, Bill?"

"Shut up, Alice."

"Then how come you won't get hard for me like you used to?"

"Because I may have to kill another son of a bitch this morning."

"Who?" Alice asked, drawing away from him.

"The bastard who brought Nellie back to Abilene, that's who," he snarled.

Alice swung her feet off the mattress, standing up to put on her clothes. "You've fallen in love with her, ain't you, Bill? I know that's what it is."

"I don't aim to talk to a two-dollar whore about it, Alice. But I'm most likely gonna have to kill this son of a bitch by the name of John Slocum."

Alice stepped into her torn dress, draping her stockings over her arm. "I'm gonna go now, Bill. You ain't wantin' me and all."

"You talk too goddamn much, Alice. If you'd shut your fucking mouth, maybe we'd get down to business."

She took a few backward steps toward the door. "Not when all you've got on your mind is Nellie Cass. You can't even fuck me hard like you used to."

"That's because you won't shut up about Nellie. What's between me an' her is our business."

"I'm real sorry, Bill, but I just don't interest you no more."

He sat up slowly to drink again. "I reckon not, Alice. Go home."

"Good night, Bill. Maybe some other time."

"Get the hell out of here, Alice. I'm tired of looking at your ugly face."

She opened her mouth to object to what he said, then she thought better of it and picked up her shoes before she left his room.

He sat, propped against the pillows for several minutes after Alice left, saying nothing, sipping from the new bottle of wine.

"I'm gonna have to kill Slocum," he muttered, as slanted rays of morning light beamed through his window. "Whoever John Slocum is, he's gonna be a dead man before the sun goes down on Abilene tonight . . ."

18

The right woman. Slocum recalled the only girl he'd known in his life who had seemed like the "right woman" at the time. It was the summer of his fourteenth birthday . . .

Not far from their Allegheny Mountains home in Calhoun County, Georgia, in an isolated valley at the end of a two-rut road across rough country, John Slocum and his brother, Robert, were fishing in a creek one day, a sunny spring day. Robert allowed as how he'd had enough of fishing and took his cane pole and tin of worms to head back to the house.

John sat on the creek bank, alone with his thoughts, until he heard a rustling in the brush nearby, his attention on a cork tied to his fishing line.

He glanced over his shoulder. Melinda Carter, a slender, freckle-faced girl from across the ridge to the south, the daughter of a sharecropper family even poorer than the Slocums, came toward him through waist-high thistles and briars.

"Seen you fishin'," she said, smiling.

At fourteen, John didn't care much for girls. He thought about them at night sometimes, but not all that often. "So? How come you had to sneak up on me like that."

"Just curious."

"Curious? Ain't you ever seen any fishin' before?"

She came to the spot where he sat with his legs dangling over the stream, wearing a dress made of floursacking and no shoes. "Curious to see what you was doin'."

"I already said I was fishin'. Ain't you got eyes in your head, Melinda?"

She sat down beside him without an invitation. Lately, it seemed her homemade dresses had begun to fill out in certain places, the swell of budding bosoms, a hint of rounding at the tops of her hips.

"I'll tell you what I was really curious about," she said in a soft voice, "but only if you'll swear on a blue robin's egg you won't tell nobody . . . not even your brother."

He sighed. "How come it's gotta be a secret?"

She looked away. " 'Cause it's somethin' real personal. If Robert knowed I was interested in . . . somethin' like this he'd tell everybody at the schoolhouse."

"What's so all-fired special about this personal thing you's so curious about?"

Melinda's face turned a shade of pink. She waited a moment before she answered him. "It's got to do with what a man an' a woman does in bed at night. Last night, I heard my ma an' pa in the bed, making funny noises. It ain't like I never heard them same noises before, only I never got so curious as I did last night."

"Hell, Melinda, everbody knows what that is. It's called bein' poked, only you're too young to know about stuff like that."

"How come I can't know about it? I'm fourteen, same

as you. Ain't that old enough? We're in the same grade at school, so it makes me old enough . . . if you know all about bein' poked. I never had nobody tell me about it before."

"Because you're a girl. Girls ain't supposed to know such grown-up things 'til they're older."

She grinned then, but still couldn't look at him, her gaze on the opposite creek bank. "I got out of bed real quiet an' I snuck over to their bedroom door. I was afraid I was gonna wake the dog up so's he'd start barkin'. I pushed the door open just a crack."

John waited several seconds, and when Melinda refused to say any more he asked, "And just what is it you saw that was so damn special?"

"You hadn't oughta be cussin'," she scolded. "What I seen was my ma bein' poked by Pa. He had his . . . tallywhacker stuck up inside her an' she was makin' the awfulest noises, like it hurt her somethin' awful."

John wagged his head, disgusted with a girl's logic. "In the first place, it ain't called a tallywhacker. And them noises your ma was makin' wasn't on account of she was hurt. Them's called pokin' sounds."

"Pokin' sounds?"

"The sounds a full-growed woman makes when she's bein' poked by a man. My ma makes 'em all the time."

"*All the time?* You're joshin' me."

"Not ALL the time. Just at night, when my pa sticks his pecker inside her."

Melinda looked at him for the first time since their discussion began. "It ain't called a pecker. You just made up that name. There's woodpeckers an' such, but that ain't what hangs down between a man's legs."

"How come you'd know, Melinda Sue Carter? You don't know shit about bein' poked or nothin' of the kind. It damn sure ain't called a tallywhacker, that's for sure.

The right word for it is pecker. I asked Pa one time. He said folks from up north call it a cock, only any fool knows a cock is a rooster. He said it was a pecker an' my pa knows all about peckers and stuff like that."

"It gets hard sometimes," Melinda said, looking off again with a darker color in her face now. "Real hard an' real big. A lot longer'n usual, too."

"All girls are dumb," John said, watching his cork again. "Everybody in Calhoun County knows a pecker gets hard when it's around a woman."

"Does yours ever get that way?" she asked in a timid voice. "I was just wonderin'."

"All the time," John answered, which was nearly the truth. "It's hard as a rock when I wake up in the morning. Same when I got to bed at night."

"Then how come you don't poke somebody so it'll go down some like it's supposed to? Soon as Pa was done pokin' Ma he took it out an' it hung down like it's supposed to, like when he goes to the outhouse to pee. Looks like if you knowed so much about it you'd poke somebody yourself, if it's like you say, hard all the time."

It was John's turn to blush. "Hadn't found but a few girls I wanted to poke. I've poked more'n my share, maybe, only it has to be a girl I've taken a notion to poke on account of she's so pretty."

"You ain't tellin' the truth. You never poked a girl in your life," she said, sounding sure of it.

"You don't know beans about me, Melinda. I've poked a whole bunch of girls."

"Name just one."

He hung his head, studying his fishing cork with more deep intent than the situation required since the fish weren't biting. "It ain't right to give off their names. I could if I wanted, but it wouldn't be the right thing to do."

"You're joshin' me again. You never poked a girl."

"Mind your own damn business, Melinda Sue. I said it wasn't proper to tell who they were."

"That's 'cause you ain't never done it."

He glared at her now, embarrassed. "You've never been poked by nobody, so how come you're such a damn expert on it?"

She waited a time before she answered him. "I've been thinkin' how it would feel. Looks like it oughta hurt some, if all tallywhackers get as big an' hard as Pa's does. It sure does look like it'd hurt."

"You gotta wait til your teats get bigger. Men don't want to poke a girl with little teats. And I just told you it ain't called a tallywhacker. It's a pecker. Peckers don't get hard unless a woman's teats are big."

"They're gettin' bigger, case you hadn't noticed. I been measurin' 'em with Ma's measurin' tape in her sewin' box."

He gave her a look of disdain. "They're still too small to make a man's pecker turn hard. Can't hardly notice 'em under that dress."

Melinda's face was almost beet red. "They're bigger'n they look. I'll show 'em to you . . . if you want."

"I wouldn't be interested in seein' small teats, Melinda. They gotta get bigger before I'd care to see 'em. You ain't old enough yet. Wait a few years and then ask me again."

"You don't want to see 'em?"

"Not any little ones. A man's pecker don't get hard unless a girl's teats are big . . . bigger'n yours, anyway."

She turned her back on him and he wondered if he'd been too tough on her. Melinda was a friend, even if she was a girl with small teats.

"Look, Melinda. You're asking about things that only a full growed woman needs to know. Wait a spell. What's the big hurry to know all about peckers and bein' poked?"

" 'Cause I been havin' dreams. I wake up in the middle of the night feelin' real strange. It's kinda hard to talk about. I get this feelin' like I want to know what a tallywhacker feels like inside me."

"You're too young to be havin' dreams like that."

"Can't help it, Johnny. I have 'em anyways, an' it seems like they come more regular than they used to."

John watched his cork idly. The fish weren't biting today and he was wasting his time fishing. "My pa says it's the devils work when a boy thinks bad thoughts. Preacher Barnes always has a sermon against sin real close to Easter. I imagine the same goes for girls."

"I was only wonderin'."

John lifted his hook from the water, finding his worm just as it was when he started fishing. "Look, Melinda. I never did mean to hurt your feelings when I said you had little teats. It comes when you get older. My pa's pecker is a helluva lot bigger than mine. Everything grows, like seeds in a garden."

"They ain't all *that* little," she protested. She turned to look at him. "I'll show you my teats if you'll show me your pecker, or whatever it is you're supposed to call it. That way, we'd know if they was both too small."

John felt a thickening, a swelling inside his pants. "I'd only do that if you showed me your teats first."

"How come I gotta be first, Johnny? Looks like if you'd poked as many girls as you say, you wouldn't mind showin' me your pecker."

"It's account of you're so young."

"I'm the same age as you . . ."

He got up slowly, winding his fishing line around the

cane pole. "Okay, Melinda. If you promise you won't tell nobody I done this with a girl young as you, I'll take down my pants and show you my pecker. But then you gotta show me those little teats. Won't be fair if I'm the only one who shows what's under my britches."

"I swear I'll do it."

He placed his cane pole on the creek bank and opened the top button on his homespun pants. "If you laugh, or tell anybody at school, I'll swear it was all a lie," he said.

"I promise I won't laugh an' I sure won't tell a soul," she said.

He pulled out his stiffening cock, holding it in the palm of his hand, strangely aroused despite Melinda being only fourteen years old and fully clothed.

"Oh my gosh!" Melinda gasped. "It's bigger'n my pa's an' his is huge."

"It ain't even all the way hard yet," John boasted, although he could feel it lengthening, throbbing.

"It's real thick too," she said, her entire face the color of a sunset, her eyes locked on his member.

"Now you gotta show me your teats. Remember? You gave me a promise you would."

Melinda stood up, slowly opening the top buttons at the front of her faded blue dress. She wriggled it off her shoulders and for a moment, John couldn't quite believe what he saw. She had rounded bosoms, much larger than her poorly made dress suggested. Her nipples were round and pink and hard.

"Maybe they are a little bigger'n I figured," he said, as his cock filled with blood. "It's hard to tell when a dress has got 'em covered."

Then Melinda pushed her dress over her hips, standing naked in front of him. "Don't make fun of me, Johnny. But I wanna see if your pecker will fit inside me the way my pa's fits inside my ma. Maybe this is what Reverend Barnes is always preachin' against on Sunday, only I'd like to see if it's gonna hurt me the way it does Ma."

"It ain't gonna hurt, Melinda, only I ain't all that sure we oughta be doin' this. You'll tell, an' we'll both get in trouble with our folks."

"I've done swore I wouldn't. It don't look like it's gonna fit anyhow."

He stepped closer to her. "Lie down in that grass under the shade of the oak tree. We can try it. If it don't fit, then at least we'll know."

She backed away from him until shade from leafy oak limbs covered the blush in her cheeks. "Okay, Johnny, but I want you to promise me you won't push it in too deep. An' if it won't fit you gotta swear you'll quit when I tell you to."

"Lie down," he said, his cock feeling as though it was on fire. "I promise I won't hurt you. I'll stop any time you say."

His pecker had fit, after a bit of work, and thus had begun his first relationship with a girl. Melinda Sue Carter had been his sweetheart for years after that. Until he went off to war.

19

When Deke began taking off her corset he found the bindings tight, too restrictive to allow his fingers room to work, and he had trouble with knots on laces across the front after placing her blouse across a straight-backed chair at one side of the bed at the Bedroom Palace. Gertrude moaned, her face illuminated by pale light from the window.

"You promised me you wouldn't do this . . ." she mumbled under the strong influence of whiskey, her words slightly mushy. He'd had to help her up the rear stairway, steadying her with an arm around her waist while she giggled over her poor balance when she lost her footing.

Deke unfastened the knot and pulled strings off the hooks holding her undergarment in place. "I promised not to make no inappropriate advances till I'd paid you. Don't you think this is appropriate, now that you got my money?"

"I thought you were a gentleman . . ." She giggled softly.

151

"I am a gentle man. I'll show you just how gentle I can be, if that's what you want."

"Your . . . cock is so big. I can feel it against my leg when you rub against me. It's so big I'm sure it will hurt. Please don't hurt me."

"I promise I'll be gentle, just a little bit of my prick at a time until you tell me when to stop."

"And what if I don't ask you to stop?" She giggled again.

He pushed the corset down, across her hips, past her knees until the garment fell at the foot of the bed. "Then I won't stop," he promised.

Her breathing became faster when his hand moved gently over the mound of soft hair at the tops of her thighs. "It feels so good when . . . you touch me, Deke. But I want you to stop. I must go home now. I ain't no regular whore an' my mother is liable to be waitin' up for me."

"You can tell your mother something unexpected came up," he said, taking her hand, placing it so her fingers curled around the thickness of his shaft where it strained against his undershorts.

A moan, a mixture of pleasure and fear, escaped her lips. "I'm real sure I ain't gonna tell my mother what it was that came up," she said in a husky voice, slowly stroking his member. "I can't tell her about *this*."

He cupped one creamy breast with a palm and gently rolled her nipple between his thumb and forefinger. She gasped and a tiny shudder coursed down the length of her body. "Oh, Deke," she whispered. "Take off your shorts so I can feel the skin of your cock with my fingers."

He obliged her while lying on his side, tossing his shorts to the floor. Her hand encircled his prick, and when it did she let out another gasp. "I've never seen . . . I've never felt one so big. Even if I was to decide to let you poke me, this wouldn't fit inside me . . . I just know it wouldn't."

He grinned. "I'd never be one to push you to such a decision, Gertrude, but let me promise you that if you did decide to let me poke you, I'll put it in real gentle, not all of it, mind you." He pinched her rosy nipple a little harder, and suddenly her spine arched off the mattress.

"It's too big around to go in at all," she groaned, fingers measuring his circumference almost unconsciously while she kept pumping up and down on his cock. "I'm afraid it'll tear me in half. I won't let you hurt me that way, but I do wish there was something we could do . . ." She trembled and fell back on the bed with a sigh, still jacking his prick, moaning, moving her head side to side on the pillow with her eyes tightly closed.

Deke put a finger between the wet lips of her cunt and gently entered her, feeling her slickness and the fever in her loins. He was sure he could work his cock into her if he did it slowly, without too much pressure right at first.

Involuntarily, she began hunching against his finger as tiny spasms gripped her thighs. "Please Deke," she whimpered. "You gotta think of something. I feel like I'm about to explode."

He withdrew his damp finger and moved carefully between her legs, placing the tip of his cock against her mound.

"No, Deke!" she cried, grinding her pelvis up and down as she held firmly to his cock with her fingers. "It's much too big to go in."

With only the slightest pressure he pushed his prick between the lips of her cunt and now, as she thrust herself against it he saw a tear glisten on her cheek.

"I want it," she whispered, "but there ain't room. You have the biggest prick . . . too big for a girl like me. I'm not very experienced, you see."

Ever so slowly he pressed his member slightly deeper until it would go no further, meeting resistance. And still, Gertrude ground her tight opening back and forth, making a wet, sucking sound when the tip of his prick went in and out.

"You must stop," she gasped, releasing her grip on his cock to encircle his buttocks with both hands, clawing fiercely into his skin with her fingernails, pulling him closer, deeper.

The difference did not escape him, her protests and her hunger for his prick, asking him to stop while she drew him closer to her, rolling her hips, thrusting forward with her wet cunt at the same time she told him to stop.

"Just a little more," he said into her ear, scenting the sweet smell of her hair, her lilac water perfume.

"No. Please no," she hissed, clenching her teeth but with an ever-increasing speed to her pelvic thrusts, again voicing a wish for him to stop while her body seemed to be demanding more of his prick. "You swore you was a gentleman—"

"I'll do it gently," he replied, pushing harder, feeling the muscles in her cunt relax, opening a fraction more to accept his cock.

"That . . . feels . . . good," she breathed, "but you gotta stop. You're hurtin' me."

"You said it felt good."

"It does. It hurts, an' it feels good. I don't understand how. Oh, please stop before you hurt me more."

Deke had known for years he would never be able to understand women. "There's such a thing as hurtin' in a good way?" he asked, pumping gently, more deeply, into her opening. Slippery sounds accompanied their every move and the heat from her cunt was like a fire now.

"Yes. I mean . . . no." Her fingernails dug deeper into his buttocks. Tiny beads of sweat formed on her brow and the cleft between her breasts.

His erection was throbbing and the warm wetness around it caused his balls to rise, spreading a warmth of their own down his thighs, across his abdomen. He could smell her sweet musk and the tremors in her limbs only added to his excitement—he pushed deeper inside her, suddenly her body went rigid underneath him.

"Now," she sighed, hammering against his shaft in spite of a lingering trace of resistance where the walls of her hungry cunt held him back. "Please stop now—"

He closed his mind to her feeble protests and thrust a half inch more of thick cock into her.

"Oh Deke . . . no more. I can't take more."

The bed began to rock, bedsprings squeaking, while the headboard tapped the wall of the room with every stroke and he was sure that any second now, his testicles would burst.

Her breathing came in short gasps and soft sounds rose in her throat. "Deke—"

Her skin had grown so clammy he found he was barely able to stay on top of her, the friction between their bodies creating more sweat, matting thick hair on his chest. Her breasts swayed with every stroke, rotating against his ribs like giant mounds of quivering custard.

Without any warning her cunt opened, and despite his promise to be gentle with her he buried his member inside her almost all the way to the hilt.

Gertrude screamed, clawing his buttocks until he felt blood run down his sides—she arched her spine, shaking violently, as the echo of her scream became a wail, then a softer groan. And all the while she continued to thrust against the base of his shaft with powerful lunges, hammering against him, his balls slapping the crack between her ass as he pounded his cock into her honeypot more rapidly.

She sure as hell don't act like no whore, he thought.

She slammed her groin into him several more times and then her entire body went rigid. She wailed, digging her heels into his calves, rising off the bed with him on top of her in spite of his weight.

As she reached her climax, his testicles spewed forth a stream of jism, and the feeling of ecstasy was so intense he let out a groan, driving his cock into her at tremendous speed and with the full force of the muscles in his hips.

"Oh God!" she shouted, cords standing out in her neck, her arms clasped around him with surprising strength for a small girl.

She collapsed on sweat-soaked bedsheets, panting, completely out of breath. Her head lolled to one side on the pillow and for a time she was motionless, her limbs falling limply on the mattress.

He spilled the rest of his jism in her as gently as he could and then halted the thrusting motion of his cock, finding he was also short of breath. Resting on his elbows so she could breathe easily, he looked down at her in the dawn light.

"You're really some special kind of woman, Gert," he said. "I never felt nothin' quite like this before."

Her eyes fluttered open. She stared at him a moment. "You bastard," she said softly. "You promised me you would stop if I asked you to."

"I meant to stop, only you felt so good . . . it felt so good bein' inside you that I couldn't help myself."

A slow smile crossed her face. "I knew you were a liar the minute I set eyes on you, when you walked in the Bull's Head. Men who lie to women have a certain look about them."

"Sorry if I disappointed you."

Her smile changed to a mock scowl. "You hurt me. Your cock was too big and you used it in me anyway."

"Like I said, I just couldn't help it. And you didn't say a man had to be perfect, did you? Sometimes women get overtook by emotion. I'm just a man, a lonely trail cowboy, an' if a beautiful woman winds up in my bed I can't always control some of my urges."

"You lied to me." She said it playfully, not with scolding in her voice.

"I forgot that promise I made in a moment of passion. I hope you won't hold it against me."

She stirred underneath him, and the movement brought a smile to her lips. The muscles in her thighs quivered. She kissed him hard across the mouth and he sensed her hunger was about to come alive again.

Very gently, he moved his prick inside her, pulling back as if he meant to withdraw. She reached for him to hold him where he was.

"Don't leave yet," she whispered. "I like the way it feels now, when your cock ain't so hard."

"I hadn't planned on leavin', darlin'. Just a change in my position, is all."

Her groin tensed and he could feel a tightening around his prick.

"I want more," she said huskily, "only please don't put it in me so deep."

He began slow strokes in and out, and now the wet, sucking sounds were louder than before with her juices mingling with his jism.

"Like that." She sighed, closing her eyes, wrapping her arms around his back.

His slow pumping aroused her further, and her limbs began to tremble again.

"Not too deep," she groaned, wincing slightly as if the pain had also reawakened within her mound.

Deke continued his shallow strokes, feeling his member thicken again, and at the same time Gertrude's cunt opened slightly to allow him to push deeper.

"Faster," she whispered in his ear, increasing the pressure of her embrace as her fingernails dug into his back. Again the bed began to squeak as their passion mounted.

"Faster," Gertrude cried, gasping, curling her legs around his to hold him in an iron grip.

He felt a pulse in his cock. Her cunt was so slippery and wet that despite his second promise not to drive his prick into her too deeply, he found himself almost out of control. When she arched her back off the mattress, seeking more of him, he obliged her and sent his prick all the way to the hilt.

"Oh yes!" Gertrude exclaimed, clawing his back fiercely. "Do it harder . . . faster."

He let go of all his reserve and began hammering his cock into her pussy, feeling the lips of her cunt stretch to accept him. Her juices flowed down his balls, warm and slick.

"Now!" she cried, rocking against him with so much force he was forced to cling to each corner of the mattress to stay atop her, seeking a grip in the bedsheet with his toes.

"Yes! Yes! Yes!" she shrieked, her body turning to stone beneath him when a second climax jolted her.

His balls erupted a few moments later, and it seemed to him that the room was spinning . . . or was it the bed?

•   •   •

He was dressing as golden sunlight poured through a window of the Bedroom Palace. He gave her a look. "You ever hear of a feller named John Slocum?" he asked.

"Ben was talkin' about him last night. He's the one who come back to Abilene with Wild Bill Hickok's woman, Nellie Cass. How come you ask?"

"He's an old friend. Any idea where he's stayin' while he's in town?"

"The Drover's, I think. Somebody said he hired a room at the Drover's. Bill's liable to kill him if he finds him with Nellie."

"Much obliged, Miss Gertrude," Deke said, starting for the door as he buckled on his gun belt. "Hope to be seein' you again real soon, after I take care of some . . . personal business."

20

Barnaby Watson was leaving the Bedroom Palace half an hour after dawn when Deke Mason came down the stairway from the top floor rooms.

Barnaby saw him and quickly turned away, recognizing him as one of the cowboys he and John Slocum had encountered at Willow Creek in the company of the girl, Nellie.

Desperately seeking to avoid any further difficulties, he made for the door until he heard a gruff voice call to him from the stairs.

"Hey you! Drummer!"

Barnaby could envision a bullet passing through his body, perhaps several of them, unless he did precisely as he was told to do.

He froze with his hand clasping the doorknob before he turned around. "Are you addressing me, sir?" he asked. "Do we know each other?" His knees felt weak, a slight tremor in them when he recalled how close this cowboy had come to drawing on Slocum when they found the four ruffians with the girl at Willow Creek yesterday.

"You know goddamn well we know each other, you son of a bitch. You was with that bounty hunter who took Nellie away from me an' the boys."

"I was merely accompanying Mr. Slocum, as Abilene was our common destination. I'd never met the man before, and I have not seen him since."

"I hear he's stayin' at the Drovers," Deke said, reaching the bottom of the stairs.

Barnaby swallowed, his mouth suddenly dry. "I don't recall exactly, however you may be correct," he said. "It seems he did ask about rooms at the Drovers, and the food, if my memory serves me well."

Deke stalked over to glare down into Barnaby's face. "I should have killed Slocum when I had the chance. Hell, I should have killed both of you. I reckon Slocum got Bob Cole. I found a fresh grave back at the water hole, an' it damn near had to be his."

"Yes," Barnaby stammered. "Your friend came back and tried to shoot Mr. Slocum."

"Tell me about it. Did this bounty hunter shoot Bob in the back?"

"Mr. Slocum invited your associate to go for his gun. When he did, Mr. Slocum killed him with a single bullet through his heart. Mr. Cole had tried to . . . slip up on us unawares while I was . . . enjoying the company of Miss Cass. Apparently, Mr. Slocum saw Mr. Cole and confronted him regarding his intentions, to see if they were honorable. Words were exchanged, harsh words I take it, only I did not hear them."

"Slocum drew first?"

"No sir. Mr. Cole, your associate, went for his pistol at Mr. Slocum's invitation."

"An' he killed Bob?"

"That is correct. Mr. Cole did not even have the opportunity to remove his pistol before Mr. Slocum shot him through the heart."

"I don't believe it, you lyin' Yankee bastard. Bob was fast as hell."

"I promise you I am telling the truth. If you will recall the earlier incident, one of your friends, someone called him Shorty, I believe, warned the rest of you that Mr. Slocum was quite an accomplished man with a sidearm."

"Ain't hardly nobody better than Bob," Deke said, hooking his thumbs in his gun belt.

"Mr. Slocum was," Barnaby replied, "and I do hope that you will remember I was only in the company of Mr. Slocum. We'd only met a few days earlier down in the Indian Nations and we agreed to share the trail to Abilene."

Deke turned his glance toward the Drovers Inn, the tallest building in this part of town. "I'll find out what room he's in," Deke muttered. "Me an' him, we got a couple of scores to settle . . . over the whore, an' him killin' Bob the way you say he done."

Barnaby slowly edged his way out on the porch in front of the Bedroom Palace, now that Deke Mason's attention was on something else, the Drovers.

Deke followed him outside and closed the door behind them, with a sideways look at Barnaby. "You right sure he's stayin' at the Drovers?" he asked. "Any sumbitch who lies to me about a real important thing like this could wind up bein' in a grave up on Boot Hill."

"I'm quite certain I'm telling you the truth as best I recall," Barnaby answered, with the hope that he had escaped any violence with this sullen fellow.

As Deke was turning for the Drovers Inn, a lanky cowboy on a dappled gray gelding rode around a street corner near the Bedroom Palace.

He stopped his horse suddenly, giving Deke a close inspection.

"Who the hell is that?" Deke asked Barnaby. "An' why the hell is he starin' at me?"

"I've never seen him before in my life," Barnaby told him. "I only come to Abilene three times a year—"

"He's wearin' a goddamn gun," Deke growled, "an' the sumbitch is lookin' this way like he aims to start some trouble with it."

Barnaby felt his fears return quickly, for the gunman on the dappled gray did appear to be staring at the front of the Bedroom Palace. "I assure you I have no idea who he is," Barnaby said in a soft voice. "And now, if you'll excuse me, I must begin making my rounds to visit my customers."

"Then get the hell out of here," Deke snapped, his eyes still fastened on the rider.

Just as he said it, the man on the gray gelding reined away toward the city marshal's office.

21

Hickok awakened with a start, reaching for a pistol at his bedside.

"Don't shoot, Marshal," Deputy Calvin Cobbs said, spreading his hands to show they were empty. "It's me, Calvin. I need to talk to you."

"What the hell's so goddamn important that you've gotta wake me up at this hour?" Hickok demanded, glancing at a clock on the wall, discovering it was only half past eight in the morning, a time when he did not want to be disturbed by anyone for any reason. He'd explained this to Calvin a dozen times . . . so what the hell was he doing here? Hickok wondered.

"Buck Smith's waitin' out in the front office," Calvin continued. "He says he's got somethin' real important to tell you, an' that it can't wait."

"Buck? Buck Smith? What the hell does that old bastard want? And just why in the hell can't it wait until I've had a few hours of sleep?"

"He says he seen one of the fellers that took Nellie out of town. The gent's back in Abilene this mornin', only I'd better let Buck tell you about it."

Hickok's brain quickly cleared of sleep fog and the remnants of too much alcohol. "Slocum. John Slocum?"

"No sir. If I got all the facts straight, John Slocum is the one who brung her back."

"Then who did Buck see?"

"He ain't real sure 'bout his name, but he was one of the four who run off with Nellie."

Hickok sat up from his mound of pillows. "Tell Buck to come on back. My head hurts. And besides, I gotta get dressed while my head's pounding. I'll listen to what he's got to say while I put my clothes on."

"Sure thing, Marshal. I'll fetch Buck back here in just a jiffy."

Calvin plodded up a hallway between jail cells while Hickok pulled on his pants, then his boots. "Son of a bitch," he said, wincing. "Feels like my skull's about to bust wide open like a ripe melon. It was that damn whore's fault. Alice made me drink too much last night."

Moments later, an elderly cowboy who worked most of the year feeding and loading cattle at the stock pens at the rail yards came into Hickok's room. He had a darkly serious look on his face.

"Mornin', Buck." Hickok sighed, reaching for his buckskin shirt. "What's this about you seeing one of the boys who carried Nellie off?"

"Seen him just now," Buck said quietly, a bit uneasy, shifting his weight from one foot to the other. "Comin' out the front of the Bedroom Palace with this gent in a fancy suit an' derby."

"Who's the bastard who took Nellie with him?" Hickok demanded as he strapped on his gun belt.

"Like I told Calvin, I ain't all that sure of his name, but I knowed he was one of 'em. He rode with Bob Cole up from San Antone in the spring an' I've seen him around town most of the summer."

"What's his goddamn name? And what does he look like?" Hickok asked, standing up on uncertain legs with his head throbbing.

"Seems like it was Deke. Deke Mason, maybe, or Deke Martin. I know for damn sure he was one of 'em who took off with your Nellie last week."

Hickok's brain was still reeling from too many bottles of wine. "Where's the son of a bitch now?"

Buck shuffled his feet again. "Can't say for sure, Marshal, but he took one look at me afore I rode off, then he started down toward the Drover's . . . in that general direction. He was out real early, so maybe he was after somethin' to eat."

Hickok poured water into a basin and splashed it across his face. He looked in a cracked mirror at his reflection, the bloodshot eyes and beard stubble. He noticed bags under his eyes and deeper wrinkles across his mouth and forehead.

He turned to speak to Buck again. "Have you seen or heard of a gent goes by the name of John Slocum?"

"Can't say as I have, Bill, although that name sure does sound familiar."

"Have you seen Nellie?"

Buck looked down at the floor. "No sir, I sure ain't, an' I only come here this mornin' to tell you 'bout this Deke feller, on account of I know how upset you was when them drovers took her south."

"I'm grateful, Buck. I'll find this Deke Martin, or Deke Mason, whoever he is."

"Just thought you oughta know, Bill. We been friends for a spell."

"I won't forget it, Buck," Hickok said, starting toward the front office. "Just remember, you've got a big favor or two coming from me. I want you to go with me, so you can show me what this gent looks like."

"I was headed for the cow pens, Bill. I was supposed to be at work in an hour."

"All you gotta do is show me who he is. Just point him out to me, so I can kill him. As soon as you point your finger at him, you can head on down to work."

Buck seemed even more uncertain, glancing sideways at Deputy Cobbs. "I reckon I can do that, Bill, only I sure don't want to get involved in no shootin' contest."

"I'll do the shooting, Buck. Just show me what the bastard looks like."

Buck nodded, then he and Calvin started up the hallway to the front office, their boots and spurs making enough noise to wake the dead, what with Hickok's ears ringing from last night's romp with Alice.

He tied his holsters to his legs, and removed the latigo hammer thongs, to be ready for a quick pull. Whoever this Deke feller was, he was about to be dead. . . . and so was John Slocum, if the bounty hunter crossed his path.

22

Deke was standing in an alley between the Alamo Saloon and a harness shop when he saw John Slocum coming down the boardwalk, then turn into a cafe called Martha's Eatery. He recognized him easily, after their confrontation at the pool at Willow Creek where he backed Deke down from a gunfight, all because of what Shorty said.

"That's where I'll gun him down," Deke muttered, "while he's havin' his breakfast eggs." He'd been thinking about that moment at the creek all the way back to Abilene, even after he found Bob Cole's grave.

Deke waited until Slocum was inside the corner cafe before he started across the road. It being early, no one was about in this part of town and it appeared Martha's had only a handful of patrons so soon after sunrise, and because the town had emptied of cowboys since the herds came in for shipment by rail up to Chicago. Most of the Texas drovers had headed home before the weather turned bad in the Nations, their pockets full of wages, or empty after too many nights in the Devil's Addition where a man could go broke in no time.

Deke crossed the road carefully, looking both ways, making sure no one saw him. He removed the hammer thong on his Colt .44. This Slocum, whether he was a bounty hunter or a railroad detective or both, wouldn't be expecting an ambush of the kind Deke had planned for him.

Someone spoke to Deke from the early dawn shadows at one end of Martha's porch, and the sound startled him so that he reached for his pistol.

"You aimin' to shoot somebody before breakfast, mister?" a phlegm-choked voice asked.

He came within a whisker of drawing his gun to shoot the man who questioned him, crouching down, seeking the source of the sound.

He saw a bearded old man sleeping on a bench in front of the Silver Dollar Saloon, next door to Martha's Eatery. His gun hand relaxed.

"What the hell is it to you, you old bastard? You damn near got yourself killed."

"Hell, I'm already dead," the man said, sitting up, swinging a wooden peg leg off the bench. "They killed the best part of me in the war."

Deke let his gun hand drop to his side. "We was damn near all in the war," he said. "Hardly anybody got out of it clean without a nick or two."

The old codger nodded, scratching through his thick gray beard. "I reckon that's the truth, stranger," he said after a bit. "But it looked to me like you was ready to go for your gun just now."

"Mind your own goddamn business." Deke said it with all the menace he could muster after a night with Gertrude, and too many glasses of liquor.

"I generally do mind my own business, mister. Make it a practice, only I couldn't help but notice that you looked like you was makin' ready to draw your gun when you come across the road just now."

Deke was distracted by the sight of a lone figure walking down Texas Street in his direction, an unwanted intrusion into his plans to kill John Slocum. The man walking toward him had long hair, hanging below his shoulders, and it was easy to see he was wearing a pair of pistols. His outline seemed vaguely familiar.

The old man resting on the bench spoke. "Yonder comes the marshal, Marshal Wild Bill Hickok, one of the most famous gunmen in the West. I'd be careful about wantin' any shootin' if I was you . . . unless you are dead set on it."

"So?" Deke pretended not to know who the marshal was, or anything about him. "Who the hell is he? Don't seem I've ever heard of him before."

"You must be new to these parts, cowboy. He's just about the fastest gun you'll ever see when it comes to a quick draw, an' he can hit what he shoots at. I sure as hell wouldn't wanna be plannin' on no gunplay with Wild Bill around . . . not unless I knowed I was real good with a pistol."

"I wasn't plannin' on no gunplay," Deke protested, his eyes glued to the marshal. He saw another man off to Hickok's left.

The old man waited a moment. "I never was one to call another man a liar, but I seen you take that piece of latigo off your pistol. A man who ain't gonna shoot nobody leaves it where it's at, the hammer string."

"Just bein' careful," Deke said, caught between his desire to kill John Slocum and the approach of Abilene's city marshal, the man who considered Nellie Cass his private woman, even if she was a crib whore. Word all over town was, Hickok had half a dozen crib whores he called his own, when he took the notion, and when he was drunk."

"Suit yourself, stranger," the man said. "Wild Bill's a bad man to tangle with. Just a piece of friendly advice to a feller who might not know who Marshal Wild Bill Hickok is. He's damn near the most famous shootist in all of Kansas Territory, an' up in Nebraska, too."

"I don't need your goddamn advice, old man. Just keep your mouth shut," Deke said, lowering his tone so no one else could hear him. The element of surprise, with either John Slocum or Bill Hickok, was important.

It seemed odd, but the old fellow chuckled. "You got worse problems than that, stranger," he said, struggling to his feet on his peg leg. "The owl hoot who just walked into that cafe could be every bit as dangerous to a man who's on the prowl after him, if that's why you got your six-gun ready just now."

"What the hell do you mean by that?" Deke asked, keeping an eye on Hickok for the moment.

"The feller who went in the cafe is John Slocum, one of the meanest sons of bitches ever to wear a Confederate uniform. If there's a match for Hickok when it comes to usin' a gun, it's Captain Slocum."

Deke was stricken with how odd it was that so many people knew about Slocum. Deke had never heard of him before, not until Shorty warned him away from attempting a fast-draw against him at Willow Creek.

"Never heard of him," Deke muttered.

The one-legged old-timer began to hobble off down the boardwalk, moving away from the front door of the cafe. "Best hope you don't git to know him no better," he said over his shoulder, his peg leg making a deep, hollow sound on the boards when he went up Texas Street.

Deke knew he would have trouble with Hickok, since the girl, Nellie, claimed to belong to the marshal. He gave it a moment's thought as Marshal Hickok came closer to Martha's Eatery. He hadn't counted on running into two men who needed killing. His mind had been on John Slocum, for what he did to Bob down at the waterhole, and someone was flanking Hickok along the boardwalks.

He decided to wait for a better opportunity to square things with Slocum, and to avoid any conflict with the city marshal. He continued across Texas Street to a shadowy spot between buildings west of the cafe.

A thought occurred to him: If he got the chance, he would gun down Hickok and be rid of his vengeance forever. Then he could take up his quarrel with Slocum when just the right opportunity came. The man with him was probably his young deputy.

Deke stepped into the shadows, with his mind made up to wait. The soft glow of lanterns inside the cafe cast golden squares of light on either side of the dark spot where he waited to see what brought the city marshal out at this hour. It was widely known that Hickok drank heavily, and on a daily basis. Since Deke had come to Abilene in the spring, he'd never seen Wild Bill out on the streets so early in the morning—only at night, when he was intoxicated, in the mood to bully some cowboy around. Something had brought him out early, and Deke wondered if it had anything to do with Nellie.

"Somethin's up," he whispered, his heavy hand clamped around the butt of his Colt. Bob Cole might have been dumb enough, or full of whiskey courage, so that he was willing to challenge this Slocum. Down deep, Deke knew he was smarter, more cautious, than his late partner. Hickok would be an easy target for an ambush if he was drunk enough, but Deke knew nothing about Slocum, only what he'd heard.

Hickok continued toward Martha's Eatery at a leisurely pace, both hands near his guns. If Deke killed the city marshal of Abilene, he'd be on the run all the way to the Red River, and perhaps beyond it.

He made up his mind to hide in the shadows and wait, to see what lured Hickok to this part of town so early in the morning. And if he got the chance, he would put a bullet through John Slocum—not for what Slocum had done to Bob Cole, necessarily, but because he missed the feel of Nellie's naked body against his, even if her hands were tied.

The peg-legged man limped past Marshal Hickok on his way up the street.

"Mornin', Marshal."

"Morning, Cookie," Hickok said, making it plain he knew the war veteran.

"What brings you out so early, Bill?"

"I'm looking for a man by the name of John Slocum. I don't reckon you'd know him."

"Sure don't, Bill."

Hickok halted in the middle of the road. "You see any tall strangers go into Martha's this morning?"

Cookie hesitated, glancing over his shoulder. "Matter of fact, I did. Seen two of 'em, in fact. Downright unusual that you would ask."

Deke saw Hickok stiffen. "Two of them?"

"Yessir. One ain't exactly no stranger. He's been around town this summer, since the herds come in."

"And the other one?"

"He went inside the cafe. Real tall feller. Wore a gun tied low on his right leg. Hair black as a crow's wing, an' a mean look on his face."

"What about the other one . . . the one you said you saw here in Abilene this summer?"

"He never went inside, Marshal. Can't say for sure exactly where he is, only he was carryin' a low-slung pistol. If I was you, I'd be real careful . . ."

23

Slocum was drinking coffee, awaiting his ham and eggs, when he saw the silhouette of a man pass by one of the side windows of the cafe. A sixth sense, one that had kept him alive during so many close scrapes during and after the war, told him that trouble was headed his way, and to be ready for it. Some inner voice warned him of danger, and he heard it plainly now as the man's shadow disappeared between the buildings.

He pushed back his chair and got up, speaking to a waitress as he made for the front door. "I'll be right back, ma'am, so don't let anything happen to my breakfast. I'm mighty hungry and I wouldn't want to miss whatever the cook back yonder has on the woodstove."

She smiled and said, "It'll be ready in a few minutes, Sir. I'll bring it out soon as it's ready."

She headed for the kitchen off the back. Only three other patrons were in the cafe this morning and they paid little attention to Slocum or his conversation with the waitress as they ate their breakfasts.

Slocum ambled to the door, his right hand near his gun, then he stepped outside, watching the corner of the building where he'd seen the man moments earlier. Early rays of sunlight from the east cast shadows in places, and he studied the dark spots a moment before going outside.

Two men were coming down the street, still several hundred yards away. One of them had shoulder-length hair, with two pistols tied around his waist. The other man appeared to be hanging back some, being careful to stay off the road where he would be more readily seen, walking a few yards behind the man strolling down the roadway.

Could be Marshal Hickok, Slocum thought, relying on nothing but the marshal's description he'd heard in the past from men who knew him personally, or those who had seen him while they were in Abilene.

Slocum focused his attention on the space between the eatery and a harness shop. Was someone waiting in the early-morning shadows to ambush the marshal? Or was someone out early, gunning for him?

He walked softly to the corner of the porch, thumbing his hat back on his head before he peered cautiously around the edge of the cafe.

A man with a gun tied to his waist was hiding in the shade from an eave. Slocum recognized him immediately, one of the four cowboys who held Nellie captive when he and Barnaby Watson chanced upon them at Willow Creek.

"Seems we've met before," Slocum said to the cowboy, soft and low, stepping off the cafe porch to square himself in front of the gunman. "You had a young woman's hands tied up the last time—"

"You bastard," the man hissed, tensing the muscles in his right arm, fingers curling near the grips of his sidearm. "You rotten son of a bitch—"

Slocum gave him a cold grin, one that did not reach

his eyes. "You know how to cuss, cowboy. If I was gonna enter a man in a cussin' contest, you'd be my pick of the litter, and you've shown you know how to take advantage of a girl. Let's see if you know how to use that gun you're wearing."

Before the last word left Slocum's mouth, Deke Mason went for his Colt, clawing it out of his holster. He brought it up much too slowly.

Slocum drew quickly, with long-practiced ease, and fired a bellowing slug into the cowboy's belly before he could swing his gun up. The echo of Slocum's gunshot echoed up and down the streets of Abilene.

The roar of Slocum's pistol filled the small space between the buildings, as Deke was lifted up on his toes by the force of impact when a .44 caliber bullet hit him.

As a reflex, Deke's trigger finger tightened and he fired a shot into the ground before he stumbled backward, arms windmilling.

Deke collapsed on his back with a grunt, his .44 falling from his fist. A dark circle of blood began to form above his belt line, darkening his shirt where a round hole pumped fluid from his shirtfront.

Slocum heard boots running in his direction from the street behind him and wheeled around quickly to cover whoever was coming his way. The man he had figured for Marshal Wild Bill Hickok came trotting toward him with both his pistols drawn and ready for action.

He didn't want trouble with the Abilene city marshal, but survival instincts brought Slocum's pistol around to cover the running man's arrival.

"Hold up, pardner!" Slocum said, aiming for the man running toward him. "This is over. I ain't looking for another gunfight so early in the morning."

Hickok came to a halt, guns trained on Slocum. "You'll be John Slocum," he said, tensed, ready for gunplay of his own if Slocum showed the inclination.

"That's right," he answered.

"You're the feller who's got Nellie . . . *my* Nellie. I heard you brought her back to town with you."

"That's true," Slocum replied. "I was neaded north in the company of a drummer, a Mr. Barnaby Watson. We came upon the waterhole at Willow Creek and found Miss Cass with her hands tied, in the company of four cowboys. One of 'em is dyin' in this alley behind me. He was waiting in ambush . . . either for me, or for you."

Hickok peered past Slocum when he heard a soft groan. "You shot him?"

"He's gutshot. Didn't have time for better aim, with him standing in the shadows the way he was. I shot at the biggest part of him I could see."

The second man who'd accompanied Hickok came up to the alley out of breath. Hickok spoke to him.

"Take a look in yonder, Buck, an' tell me if that gent is one of the men who took Nellie."

The man he called Buck was very cautious, walking around the smoking barrel of Slocum's pistol to peer into the space between the cafe and the harness shop. The gunshot had begun to bring people out of Martha's Eatery and other business establishments in this end of town.

"That's him, Marshal," Buck said. "His name's Deke . . . either it's Mason, or Martin. He was one of the fellers who took Nellie with 'em back to Texas."

Hickok stared into Slocum's eyes and the barrel of his gun. "How'd you get her away from 'em and why?" he wondered out loud, as more people came toward the scene of the shooting.

"It's simple. Her hands were tied, and it was real plain she didn't want to be there."

Hickok continued to stare at Slocum. "A drover told me you shot Bob Cole over it."

"I killed a gunman at the creek. Can't recall his name just now, but he tried to slip up behind me and the drummer so's he could get the girl back. I saw him and let him have the first pull. He was slow. I buried him beside the creek."

Hickok lowered his pistols, letting them dangle at his sides while he considered Slocum. "You must be mighty damn good with a six-gun, Slocum."

"I get by. I'm still alive."

"I figure you know I'm city marshal of Abilene," Hickok said as he holstered his twin Colts.

"I haven't broken any laws here, Marshal. I killed a man in self-defense down at the creek, and this dumb son of a bitch was crazy enough to draw on me first. Had no choice but to shoot him the way I did."

Hickok wagged his head. "You won't be charged with a damn thing, Mr. Slocum. In fact, I'm damn glad you got this son of a bitch. But there's one more question to be answered."

"And what is that, Marshal?"

"What about Nellie? Where is she? And how come she's with you?"

"She wants to leave Abilene. She told me about the money she owed you, and I gave it to her. She'll repay her debt to you this morning."

"Then she's staying in Abilene?"

"No, Marshal, she ain't. She wants to leave this town, and I told her I'd take her as far as I was going, up to Denver, and then I'd see to it that she got on a train."

"How come you're being so goddamn generous to a whore, Mr. Slocum?"

"She's really only a girl. Hard times forced her into a hard business."

"What if I told you I ain't gonna let you take her with you?" Hickok asked, setting his jaw a little.

Slocum holstered his own gun. "I reckon I'd have to wire an old friend at the United States Marshals office in Denver, to see if a woman can be held in a town against her will. I've known Sam for a long time, a dozen years. I 'spect he'd come down real quick if I asked him to, in order to investigate."

Hickok's shoulders seemed to slump. He looked around him at the small crowd drawn to the shooting. "Go ahead and take her then, Slocum," he said. "Just make damn sure she pays me that eight dollars she owes me."

"I'm sure she will," Slocum replied.

Hickok turned to Buck. "Go fetch Doc Green. That sorry son of a bitch groanin' in the alley might live long enough for me to see him hung."

Buck nodded and turned around, lumbering back up Texas Street in boots and spurs.

Hickok gave Slocum the eye one more time, cocking his head as if he wasn't quite sure what to make of him. "I'd heard you was a bounty hunter and a railroad detective, Slocum, and that you knew your way around a gun. Appears most of what I was told is true."

"I get along, for the most part," Slocum said.

"If that sumbitch pissing and moaning back there next to the cafe was layin' in ambush for me, I owe you a favor. But if he was after you instead, seems he made a helluva mistake."

Slocum nodded to the marshal. "Either way, it's over. The guy I shot won't live long, and I killed one of his partners down at the water hole. If you have any doubts about how it happened, speak to Mr. Barnaby Watson. He told me he'd be staying over at the Bedroom Palace."

"Won't be no need," Hickok said. "I figure Kansas is a better place without either one of 'em. Don't make a damn bit of difference how they died."

Hickok started back toward his office, then he stopped and gave Slocum a look. "Make sure Nellie gives me that money before you take her to Denver." He hesitated. "And take care of her. She ain't no bad woman . . . not really. Kinda had a tough upbringing when she was younger."

"I'll see that she gets to Denver safely, Marshal. You're right about it . . . she's not like the others in the district. I think she did the only thing she could to survive."

Hickok chuckled. "Hell, we're all the same when it comes to that. Be seein' you, John Slocum. Glad we didn't have to find out which one of us was faster with a gun . . ."

With his bay horse loaded in a railroad cattle car, Slocum and Nellie boarded the Kansas and Pacific for Denver that afternoon. Nellie wore a new pink dress and new black high-button shoes.

They took seats in a passenger car as the engineer sounded his whistle. Nellie smiled and rested her head against his shoulder.

"Wild Bill never said a word when I handed him the money," she said, glancing out the passenger car window.

"I didn't figure he would," Slocum replied, as the hiss of released steam brakes sounded up and down the train.

"I won't never forget what you've done for me," Nellie told him.

He grinned as the train began to chug away from the Abilene depot. "I'll give you a chance to show me you're grateful when we get to Denver," he said.

"You can count on it," she whispered, as the bleak cattle pens and the outline of Abilene's houses and business district began to fall away behind the moving train.

A Valentine's Surprise

READ ALL THE CANDY FAIRIES BOOKS!

Chocolate Dreams

Rainbow Swirl

Caramel Moon

Cool Mint

Magic Hearts

Gooey Goblins

The Sugar Ball

COMING SOON:

Bubble Gum Rescue

Double Dip

Candy Fairies

A Valentine's Surprise

HELEN PERELMAN

ILLUSTRATED BY
ERICA-JANE WATERS

ALADDIN
NEW YORK   LONDON   TORONTO   SYDNEY   NEW DELHI

ALADDIN

An imprint of Simon & Schuster Children's Publishing Division

1230 Avenue of the Americas, New York, NY 10020

First Aladdin paperback edition December 2011

Text copyright © 2011 by Helen Perelman Bernstein

Illustrations copyright © 2011 by Erica-Jane Waters

ALADDIN is a trademark of Simon & Schuster, Inc., and related logo is a registered trademark of Simon & Schuster, Inc.

For information about special discounts for bulk purchases, please contact Simon & Schuster Special Sales at 1-866-506-1949 or business@simonandschuster.com.

The Simon & Schuster Speakers Bureau can bring authors to your live event. For more information or to book an event contact the Simon & Schuster Speakers Bureau at 1-866-248-3049 or visit our website at www.simonspeakers.com.

Designed by Karina Granda

The text of this book was set in Berthold Baskerville Book.

Manufactured in the United States of America 0312 OFF

4 6 8 10 9 7 5 3

Library of Congress Control Number 2011920262

ISBN 978-1-4424-2215-5

ISBN 978-1-4424-2216-2 (eBook)

For Sarah Collier, a sweet and true fan

Contents

1

Supersweet Surprise

Raina the Gummy Fairy sprinkled handfuls of colorful flavor flakes into Gummy Lake. She smiled as the gummy fish swam over and gobbled up the food. Watching the fish eat made Raina's tummy rumble. She had gotten up very early and had been working in Gummy Forest all morning. When she settled on a perch high up on a gummy tree, Raina opened her back-pack. All the animals in the forest were fed, and now she could relax and eat her own lunch.

Raina had an important job in Sugar Valley. She took care of the gummy animals that lived in Gummy Forest. There were many types of gummy animals, from friendly bear cubs to playful bunnies. Raina was fair and kind to each of the animals—and they all loved her.

"Hi, Raina!" a voice called out.

Raina looked up to see Dash, a Mint Fairy, flying in circles above her head. The small, sweet fairy glided down to see her.

"I was hoping to find you here," Dash said. "I need your help."

Raina was always willing to help out any

of her friends. She had a heart that was pure sugar. "What's going on?" she asked.

Dash landed on the branch next to Raina. She peered over at the bowl in Raina's hand. Dash was small, but she always had a huge appetite!

"Hmmm, that smells good," she said. "What is that?"

"It's fruit nectar. Berry brought me some yesterday," Raina told her. She watched Dash's eyes grow wider. It wasn't hard to tell that Dash would love a taste. "Do you want to try some?" she asked.

"Thanks," Dash said, licking her lips. "Berry's nectars are always supersweet." Dash leaned over for her taste. Berry the Fruit Fairy had a flair for the fabulous. And she could whip up a spectacular nectar. "Yum," Dash continued. "Berry makes the best fruit nectar soup."

Raina laughed. "I don't think I've ever heard you say that you didn't like something a Candy Fairy made," she told her minty friend.

"Very funny," Dash said, knowing that her friend was speaking the truth.

"Have you come up with any ideas about what to get Berry?" Raina asked.

Dash flapped her wings. "That is why I'm coming to see you," she said. "I was hoping you could give me an idea. I know Berry would love something from Meringue Island, but that is a little too far. She's the only one I haven't gotten a gift for, and Valentine's Day is tomorrow. Since it's also her birthday, I want to make sure the gift is supersweet."

"Sure as sugar, Berry would love anything from Meringue Island," Raina agreed. Meringue Island was in the Vanilla Sea and was *the* place for fashion. Berry loved fashion—especially jewelry and fancy clothes. When Fruli, a Fruit Fairy, had come to Sugar Valley from the island, Berry was very jealous of her. Fruli had beautiful clothes and knew how to put together high-fashion looks.

"The truth is," Raina added, leaning in closer to Dash. "Berry would like anything you gave her."

"But I want to give her something she is really going to love," Dash replied. She swung her legs back and forth. "I want to surprise her with a special gift this year." Her silver wings flapped quickly. "I wish I could think of something with extra sugar!"

"I know how you feel," Raina said. "I've had

the hardest time coming up with an idea." She looked over at Dash. "I'll tell you what I'm going to get her, but please keep it a secret."

"Sure as sugar!" Dash exclaimed. She clapped her hands. "Oh, what are you planning?"

Raina took her last sip of the fruit nectar. "Last night I was reading a story in the Fairy Code Book, and I got a delicious idea."

Dash rolled her eyes. "I should have guessed that this would have something to do with the Fairy Code Book," she said.

Raina read the Fairy Code Book so often that her friends teased her that she knew the whole book by heart.

"Well," Raina continued, "there is a great story in the book about Lyra, the Fruit Chew Meadow unicorn."

"Oh, I love Lyra," Dash sang out. "She grows those gorgeous candy flowers at the edge of the meadow." Just as she said those words, Dash knew why Raina's grin was so wide. "You talked to Lyra, and she is going to give you a special flower for Berry?"

Raina laughed. "Dash!" she said. "You ruined my surprise." She put her empty bowl back inside her bag. "I thought that if I got Berry a flower, I could make a headband for her. You know how she loves to accessorize."

"The more the better, for Berry," Dash added. "And those are the fanciest flowers in the kingdom. *So mint!* Berry is going to love that headband." Dash stopped talking for a moment to take in the whole idea. "Wait, how'd you get

Lyra to do that for you? Unicorns don't like to talk to anyone!"

Raina smiled. "Well, that's not really true," she said.

"Let me guess," Dash said. "Did you read that in a book?"

Raina giggled. "Actually, I didn't," she told her friend. "To be honest, I think Lyra is just shy."

"Really?" Dash asked. "Can I meet her? Maybe she'll have another idea for a gift for Berry. Let's go now." She stood up and leaped off the branch into the air.

"I've been working all morning," Raina said. She reached her arms up into a wide stretch. "Maybe we can go in a little while?"

Dash fluttered back down to the branch. Her

small silver wings flapped quickly. "Come on," she begged. "Let's go now!"

Dash was known for being fast on the slopes of the Frosted Mountains—and for being impatient. She liked to move quickly and make fast decisions.

Leaning back on the gummy tree, Raina closed her eyes. "Please just let me rest a little, and then we can go," she said with a yawn.

"All right," Dash said. "Do you have any more of that nectar?"

Raina gave Dash her bowl and poured out some more of Berry's nectar. Then she shut her eyes. Before Raina drifted off to sleep, she imagined Berry's happy face when she saw her birthday present. Sure as sugar, Valentine's Day was going to be supersweet!

2

Sweet Lyra

After Raina woke up from her nap, she and Dash flew to Fruit Chew Meadow. The meadow was on the other side of Candy Castle and wasn't that far away from Gummy Forest. Raina knew that with Dash, the trip would go fast. Dash was a champion at sledding and loved to fly down the slopes of the Frosted Mountains and

Marshmallow Marsh on her sled. Raina usually preferred to take her time. She liked to see the colorful sights of Sugar Valley and enjoy all the delicious scents blowing in the breeze. Today, however, she was ready to race Dash to Fruit Chew Meadow.

"I can't believe I'm keeping up with you," Raina called over to Dash.

Dash smiled. "I'm glad you *are* going fast. I can't wait to talk to Lyra!"

Laughing, Raina shook her head. Her minty friend always wanted a speedy answer. Raina flapped her wings. She was excited to see the flower that Lyra had for her.

"I thought unicorns were a little sticky when it came to being around fairies," Dash said.

"Not Lyra," Raina said. "She's not like that

at all. Besides, Lyra likes Berry very much. She wants to help make her birthday special."

"Berry is going to be so happy!" Dash said, smiling.

Now that Candy Castle was behind them, Fruit Chew Meadow was just ahead. The fairies flapped their wings faster and giggled as they headed toward the ground. As they drew closer, Raina stopped laughing and squinted her eyes. Normally, the far end of Fruit Chew Meadow was full of flowers. The bright rainbow of colorful flowers was always such a breathtaking sight. But today the field looked different.

"Oh no!" Raina gasped. Her wings slowed as she glided above the meadow. Usually, the tall candy flowers were reaching up to the sky, but now they were dragging on the ground.

"Holy peppermint," Dash mumbled as she flew closer to the field. "These flowers look awful."

"What happened?" Raina said. She hovered above the ground, staring at the sad-looking flowers. "This must have just happened. We would have heard of this for sure."

"Sour news travels fast," Dash agreed. "I'm sure Princess Lolli doesn't even know about this, otherwise she would be here now."

Princess Lolli was the fairy princess who ruled over Sugar Valley. She was fair and true and always helped out the fairies when there was trouble.

"I wonder if anyone else knows about this," Dash said. She spun around. "Do you see Lyra anywhere?"

Raina held her hand over her eyes to shield the sun. She scanned the meadow. "I don't see her. We have to find her." She flapped her wings and flew up to see better. "Lyra's usually right here near the berry cherry tree," she said. "I wonder where she could be." She looked over at Dash.

"I don't have a good feeling about this," Dash said. She wrinkled her nose. "Something smells sour here."

"Well," Raina said, trying to stay calm. "Let's look for clues. That's always the best way to solve a mystery."

The two fairies hovered above the meadow and searched.

"Poor Lyra," Dash said. "This must have happened after all the Fruit Fairies left this morning."

Raina nodded. "You must be right," she said. "The Fruit Fairies would have helped. Keep looking!"

As Raina flew over the meadow she wasn't sure what she was looking for. Lyra was a large white unicorn with a rainbow horn that glowed. There weren't many places for an animal that size to hide in the meadow.

"Wait!" Raina said. She flew down to the ground and squatted low on the grass. Dash followed close behind her.

"Lyra's hoofprints!" Raina exclaimed. She pointed to a dirt path and a small hoofprint. "If we follow these, maybe we can find her."

The two fairies followed the hoofprint clues. Near the edge of the meadow they found the unicorn.

"Oh, Lyra!" Raina cried out. She saw the beautiful white unicorn lying down behind a berry thistle and rushed toward her.

Lyra was lying on her side. Her normally bright rainbow horn was dull and nearly wiped of color.

Raina sat by Lyra's head and stroked her nose. "Lyra, are you okay?" she whispered softly in her ear.

There was no answer.

"Lyra," Raina begged. "Please answer me. What happened?"

Dash sat down on the other side of Lyra's head. She rubbed her silky white neck "Lyra, can you hear us?" she asked.

Lyra's eyes fluttered slightly.

"She looks very weak," Dash added. "Poor

Lyra!" She bent down to get a closer look at the unicorn. "She's really sick."

Raina knew they had to do something—and fast. It was hard to tell just how long Lyra had been lying there. And her dull horn was very upsetting. "We need all of us together to solve this problem," she said.

Lyra's eyes fluttered again. The unicorn's long lashes seemed too heavy to let her keep her eyes open.

"It's all right," Raina told her. She patted Lyra gently. "We're going to get you some help," she whispered in her ear.

"And try to figure out what went on here," Dash added.

Raina stood up and looked around. The field seemed so strange without the tall stalks of colorful flowers. "Maybe she hurt herself," she said softly. She looked over Lyra's white body, but the unicorn appeared unharmed.

"We can't move her by ourselves," Dash said. Lyra was a full-sized unicorn and much too large for just two Candy Fairies to pick up.

Raina knew Dash was right. "Let's send sugar flies to our friends. If we're all together, we can come up with a plan."

The fastest way to get information around Sugar Valley was to send a sugar fly note. Those little flies could spread news faster than anyone.

Poor, sweet Lyra, Raina thought. *How did this happen to you?*

Raina touched the unicorn's horn and closed her eyes. She wished she could help the gentle creature and find out what had made her so sick.

3

A Sour Mystery

Raina and Dash sat by Lyra's side. The unicorn seemed to be resting, but she was weak and her horn was still dull. Raina didn't like seeing the unicorn so sick.

"Let's try to make Lyra more comfortable," Raina said. She gathered some soft fruit chews and put them under Lyra's head. "Oh, I hope the others get here soon!" she said, looking up at the sky.

"Let's tell everyone that we were working on a special candy for Princess Lolli," Dash said. "I don't want to give away Berry's surprise gift. She'll figure out that we were up to something."

"Maybe," Raina said. "But then there will be questions about the special candy." She reached over and pet Lyra. She felt very warm. "Telling one little lie doesn't seem bad, but one lie always leads to many, many more."

Dash agreed. "You're right. We'll just say that we came to see Lyra. Everyone will be thinking about how to help her."

Putting her head close to Lyra's nose, Raina listened carefully. "She's barely breathing," she told Dash.

"Look!" Dash cried. "I see Melli and Cocoa!"

Up in the sky the Caramel Fairy and Chocolate Fairy were headed toward them. Raina waved. Just as they landed Berry flew in beside them.

"Sour strawberries!" Berry exclaimed. "What happened here?" She bent down to Lyra. "I was just here this morning and Lyra was fine. Oh, the poor thing." Gently she stroked the sleeping unicorn's neck.

"Sweet Lyra," Melli sighed.

"She doesn't look well," Cocoa added. She glanced around at all the wilted flowers in the meadow. "Melli and I were nearby around lunchtime, and the flowers were standing tall. So Lyra couldn't have been lying here for long."

"Oh, Lyra," Berry cooed. She sat down close

to her. "Sour sugars! Look at her horn!" Berry looked at Raina. "Her magic!"

"We have to get her some help," Raina said. She was trying very hard to remain calm.

"Unicorns hold all their magic in their horn," Berry blurted out. "Lyra must be very sick if her horn is so dull."

Raina lowered her eyes. She was aware of that fact, but she had been too worried to say those words out loud.

Melli paced around Lyra. "Oh, this is awful. And a mystery."

"A sour mystery," Dash mumbled.

Cocoa flew up in the air and scanned the meadow. "All of Lyra's flowers are drooping. Whatever is affecting her is affecting the whole meadow."

"The flowers respond to Lyra," Berry said. "If she doesn't have her magic and she can't sing, the flowers will die." Berry's wings began to move. "We have to do something fast."

Raina put her hand on Berry's shoulder. "That is why we called you all here."

"Let me stay with Lyra," Berry said. She reached in her bag for some fruit nectar. "Maybe she'll have some." She held the food out to the unicorn, but there was no movement.

"She's so weak," Melli said sadly.

Raina's eyes were brimming with tears. She knew that she had to be strong. "Berry, you stay with Lyra and keep her calm. The rest of us will search the meadow. We'll look for clues."

The fairies all agreed. Berry stayed with Lyra as Raina, Dash, Melli, and Cocoa flew back and forth over the meadow. Overall, the meadow didn't look disturbed . . . except for the wilted flowers.

"Holy peppermint!" Dash cried out. She waved her friends over to the edge of the meadow. She zoomed down to the ground and then signaled her friends to follow.

"A broken fence!" Raina exclaimed. She landed beside Dash, the others right behind her.

The thick caramel fence surrounding one of the flower beds was broken.

"Those fences are incredibly strong," Melli said. She bent down to examine the break. "That caramel is hard to crack."

Cocoa ducked down low to get a better view. "Well, something—or someone—broke the fence."

Dash sat down on the ground and put her head in her hands. As she stared at the broken fence her nose began to twitch. She put her hand on the ground and then up to her mouth. "Holy peppermint!" she said softly. "There's salt all over the ground here." She stood up and began to follow the path while the others watched her with puzzled expressions. Suddenly Dash bent down, scooped something up in her hand, and then she showed it to her friends.

"Salt?" Melli asked. "How could there be salt here? Everyone knows . . ."

Before she could finish her sentence, her friends were around her. Melli had her hand in front of her mouth. She couldn't bear to say the words.

"Salt is poisonous for unicorns!" Raina blurted out.

"Mogu! That salty old troll," Cocoa hissed.

"No wonder Lyra is weak and sick," Melli said softly.

Dash was so angry her wings flapped and took her up off the ground. "Mogu has been coming to the meadow to steal candy! And his salty tracks have harmed Lyra. This is so sour—even for Mogu."

"You really think Mogu would hurt Lyra?" Raina asked. "Even for a troll that would be superbitter."

"Maybe he didn't realize the salt was harmful to Lyra," Melli offered.

"Not likely," Cocoa muttered. "He saw a broken fence as an invitation."

"Sweet sugar," Raina gasped. "We need to get Lyra stronger so that she can sing and get back to guarding the meadow." She looked at her friends. "And we need to tell Berry. She's not going to handle this well."

"And Berry's birthday is tomorrow," Melli added sadly. "This doesn't seem like a time for celebrating at all."

Raina took a deep breath. "Dash and I came here to get one of Lyra's flowers so we could make Berry's birthday gift extra-sweet." Raina looked over at Fruit Chew Meadow and sighed. "We still have time to solve this mystery and to make Berry's birthday *and* Valentine's Day special." She looked at the worried expressions on her friends' faces. "We have to at least try."

CHAPTER 4

A Salty Problem

When the four friends returned to the far end of Fruit Chew Meadow, Berry was still sitting next to Lyra. The unicorn had not moved since they had left. Berry was stroking Lyra's neck and singing softly.

"Gentle breeze and sweet light," Berry sang out,

"How is Lyra?" Raina asked, kneeling beside her friend. The white unicorn was still asleep and her horn was still dull. Not a trace was visible of the colors that normally glowed from her horn. "Did she wake up?"

"Yes, she took a few sips of the nectar but then dozed off again," Berry said. "Did you find any clues?"

Raina decided not to sugarcoat the truth. "We found a broken fence and a trail of salt," she told her.

"Salt?!" Berry exclaimed. Her eyes were wide and full of concern.

Raina knew that Berry was aware of the dangers of salt in the meadow.

"Oh, this is worse than we thought," Berry said softly. She looked into Raina's eyes. "It's Mogu, isn't it?"

"We're not sure," Raina told Berry. "But the first thing we need to do is get rid of the salt. If we can clear the area, maybe Lyra will be able to speak to us and tell us what happened."

"Let's try to wash all the flowers off," Berry said.

Raina smiled at her Fruit Fairy friend. "That's what I thought too. We'll make a spring rain to take the salt away. We can go to Red Licorice Lake for the water."

"I'll stay with Lyra," Berry offered. She looked down at the gentle unicorn. "She seems to do better when I sing to her."

Raina gave her friend a quick hug. "That is a great idea," she said. "You stay here."

The four fairies flew down to the shores of Red Licorice Lake. They each grabbed a bucket from a nearby shed. Buckets were kept there in case of droughts or other emergencies.

This is definitely an emergency, thought Raina.

"Once the salt is gone, Lyra will feel better, right?" Dash asked Raina as she filled up her bucket.

"I hope so," Raina replied. She didn't know for sure, but she knew that the salt was causing Lyra to grow weak and sick. "Come, let's hurry," she urged her friends.

Together, the fairies flew up and down the meadow. They poured the water over the wilted

flowers and washed the white salt away. With each trip to the lake, the salt was slowly disappearing. It took many trips and bucketfuls of water, but soon the wet meadow didn't have a trace of salt.

Then the fairies gathered back around Lyra and Berry.

"How is Lyra?" Raina asked as they flew up.

"She's a little better," Berry told her. "Getting rid of the salt has helped. I can see she's a little stronger."

"This still doesn't make sense to me," Raina said. She sat down next to Berry, tapping her finger to her head. "Mogu is afraid of Lyra. Why would he even come here?"

"Who would be afraid of a sweet unicorn?" Dash asked.

"When it comes to Mogu, there isn't always a solid reason," Berry told her.

"I remember those tall stalks of salty pretzels in Black Licorice Swamp," Cocoa told her friends. "If there is salt here, I'm sure it's because of Mogu and the Chuchies."

Raina knew that Cocoa was remembering the time when she flew to Black Licorice Swamp. Mogu and his mischievous companions, the Chuchies, had stolen her chocolate eggs. Cocoa had tricked Mogu into giving them back. The Chocolate Fairy knew all about the troll's salty ways.

"If there is salt here, Mogu is probably to blame," Cocoa said again. "His greed will drive him to do anything." Thinking of her chocolate eggs made Cocoa stamp her foot. "We have to trick Mogu again," she said. "Cleaning up the meadow may solve the problem for now, but that troll will be back."

"Especially if Lyra isn't guarding the flowers," Melli added. "There's nothing here to stop him."

"We're here now," Raina said bravely. "It's sticky business to trick a troll," she reminded her friends. She reached into her bag. "I know I've heard a story about Mogu and Lyra. Maybe there's a clue in a story that can help us."

Raina took out her Fairy Code Book and thumbed through the pages.

Dash sat down next to her. "I can't imagine Mogu being afraid of anything."

Flipping through the book, Raina agreed. "Yes, yes, I'm sure I've read a story in here about Mogu and Lyra. I think it was about Lyra's pointy horn."

Laughing, Berry slapped her hand to her knee. "I bet that horn can come in handy when dealing with Mogu," she said, giggling.

"What is the story?" Dash asked. She was growing impatient.

"Mogu was once pricked by Lyra's horn when he tried to steal her fruit-chew flowers," Raina read from the thick book. She turned the book around to show her friends the picture. "I knew there was a story!"

"Ha!" Dash burst out. "Look at that!" She pointed to a picture of Mogu with a tear in his pants. Sticking out of the hole was Mogu's polka-dotted underwear. "No wonder Mogu is afraid of Lyra. She totally embarrassed him!"

"You should really read the Fairy Code Book more often," Raina scolded her friends.

"We don't have to," Berry said, smiling. "We have you! You remember every story."

Melli put her arm around Raina. "And it's a good thing, too," she said. "Raina, what would we do without you?"

Blushing, Raina turned the page. "This was many years ago, and Mogu has not been back here since. I wonder what made him come back now."

"Maybe he just wanted to have a fruit-chew flower," Berry offered. "They are the sweetest in Sugar Valley."

Raina looked over at Dash. She didn't want her to say anything about the gift for Berry. She caught Dash's eye. Dash immediately understood and bit her lip. It was hard for Dash not to speak her mind!

"Or maybe he heard about the broken fence

and thought he could slip in unnoticed," Dash said.

"Who knows why a salty old troll does anything," Melli said. She got up and paced around in a circle.

Berry rubbed Lyra's dull horn. "Lyra needs help," she said. "Cleaning the meadow is not going to wash this problem away."

Raina hugged the Fairy Code Book close to her chest. Normally, reading a story helped her decide the right thing to do. But this tale offered little advice. All she knew for sure was that Lyra was not better. Berry was right, just washing the meadow wasn't going to solve the problem. If they were going to help Lyra, they had to come up with a plan to stop Mogu. And to get Lyra well again.

And that was a salty problem she had no idea how to solve.

5

Burst of Hope

Raina and Berry huddled together on a blanket in Fruit Chew Meadow. Normally, Raina would have loved to spend time hanging out with Berry. Only now they were both worried about Lyra. Lyra had been resting under Berry's pink cotton-candy shawl, but she still looked very weak. The others had flown off to get some food for dinner. Raina was having a hard time keeping still. Her wings were fluttering and she was twisting her long hair around her finger.

"You're worried about Lyra, aren't you?" Berry asked.

"Yes," Raina said. But she couldn't tell Berry that Lyra was not all she was concerned about. She also didn't want to ruin Berry's birthday with this sour event. With the look of things now, it didn't seem that Lyra would be getting better by Sun Dip. Normally, Sun Dip was a festive time of day when fairies would gather. The sun would slide behind the Frosted Mountains and the sky would turn deep pinks and purples. Fairies would share sweet treats and talk with friends. But today when the sun went down, there'd be little Raina and her friends would want to celebrate.

Raina touched the Fairy Code Book in her bag. She wished the story about Mogu and Lyra had helped her come up with a plan. She sighed.

"Mogu has a way of ruining sweet times in Sugar Valley," Berry said softly. She leaned forward to pet Lyra. "Please, Lyra, take some nectar. It will make your throat feel better. We all need you to sing."

Raina blew her bangs off her forehead. Lyra was not getting stronger, even though all the salt had been washed away. They were going to have to move her. "How are we going to move a unicorn?" Raina asked.

"We've brought food," Cocoa called from above.

"I'm not really hungry," Raina replied.

"Me neither," Berry told Cocoa.

Cocoa, Melli, and Dash came to sit on the blanket. They spread out the food for their friends.

"We should eat," Melli said. "Then we can think of a solid plan."

Dash looked around at the pale, wilted flowers. "What do you think will happen to the flowers if Lyra's voice doesn't come back?" she asked.

Raina lowered her head. "I'm not sure," she said. "I don't think the flowers will survive. Already they look even less colorful, and it's only been a few hours."

"The greatest present for my birthday would be if Lyra would get better," Berry mumbled.

Hoping that she could make her friend's wish come true, Raina gave Berry a tight squeeze.

"We still have time," she said, trying to believe her words would come true.

A gentle breeze ruffled the grass. Above them Raina spotted a sweet sight. "Oh, Berry!" she cried out. "It's Princess Lolli!"

In a flash, Princess Lolli was standing before them. Her long strawberry-blond hair hung down at her shoulders, and a small candy-jeweled tiara sat on top of her head. She smoothed her bright pink dress with her hands and smiled at the young fairies. "Hello, fairies," she said. "I heard that Lyra is not well. I am so glad you are here with her."

"I don't think we've helped her much," Berry said sadly. "She is still very weak."

"Lyra can't sing," Raina said, stepping forward. "We found a broken fence and salt. We washed

the flowers and tried to get Lyra to drink some nectar. Nothing seems to be working."

"Salt?" Princess Lolli said. Her smile melted into a frown. "I was afraid that was the case."

"Do you think Mogu was here?" Cocoa asked.

"I'm not sure," the princess said. "I do know that Lyra needs some help. Let's get her to Candy Castle."

Raina bent down low to Lyra. "She can't even open her eyes. She's so weak," she said. "Lyra can't fly. How can we get her to Candy Castle?"

Everyone looked at one another.

"Bitter mint," Dash mumbled. "This is a super minty problem. Without Lyra's glowing horn, she can't fly. She's out of the race."

"That's it!" Raina shouted. Her wings flapped happily, and she rushed over to give Dash a hug.

"What?" Dash gasped.

Raina grinned at her friend. "I know exactly what we need to do," she told her friends. "I'm sure this will work!"

For the first time since they had arrived at Fruit Chew Meadow, Raina suddenly had a burst of hope.

6

Sweet and Strong

Raina was grinning while her friends gazed at her. Their mouths were open and their eyes wide.

"You really think that will work?" Cocoa asked.

Melli bit her lower lip. "Sweet caramel, Raina," she muttered. "I'm not sure we could pull that off."

"Sure as sugar, we can!" Raina exclaimed. She stood up straight, with her hands on her hips. "We have Dash, the best sled racer in Sugar Valley. We'll make a sled mint enough for a sweet unicorn. If Lyra can't fly, we'll have to pull her to Candy Castle."

Princess Lolli smiled. "Raina, that is an excellent idea," she said. "If there are any fairies who can make this happen, I believe those fairies are right here in front of me now."

"What about Mogu?" Dash asked. "What if he comes back?"

"We'll have to wait to deal with Mogu," Princess Lolli told the fairies. "First we must help Lyra." She bent down to the unicorn and whispered in her ear. Lyra slowly opened her eyes. Princess Lolli took a pink sugar cube from her

pocket and held it out to Lyra. The unicorn took the sweet treat and then closed her eyes again. Standing up, Princess Lolli faced the fairies. "I will head back to the castle to make arrangements for Lyra. I will see you all shortly."

The fairies waved good-bye to Princess Lolli. They were so thankful that she had come, but now they had work to do! If they were going to build a sled big enough for a unicorn, they had to work quickly.

Raina opened the Fairy Code Book. She put the book down on the ground for everyone to see. "Look, there's a picture of a large sled," she said. "This sled was for Mooco the chocolate cow, when she was stuck in the terrible winter storm last year in Chocolate Woods." She held up the book to show her friends the illustration.

"Hot chocolate!" Cocoa shouted. "I remember that storm. That poor cow was stuck in the thick frozen chocolate. It took every Chocolate Fairy's help to get her out."

"I think we can use this picture of a large sled to help us," Raina said. "If the Chocolate Fairies could move Mooco, we can move Lyra." She turned to Dash. "What do you think? Can we make a sled big enough for Lyra?"

Dash leaned over to see the picture. "Sure as sugar," she replied. She smiled at Raina. "Just as Princess Lolli said, we are the fairies for the job!"

Raina was thankful for the Mint Fairy's enthusiasm. She knew she could always count on Dash.

"We'll need a few supplies," Dash said. She started to pace back and forth as she thought out loud. "We'll need some fruit leather, red licorice, and something to hold the sled together."

"What about hot caramel?" Melli asked. "When the sticky syrup dries, it should hold the sled together."

"Thanks, Melli. I think you're right," Dash said. "The hot caramel is a smart choice."

Berry leaped up. "I can get the fruit leather," she said. "We'll need wide strips, and I know where to get good, strong pieces."

"I can get the licorice," Cocoa offered.

"I'll head to the Frosted Mountains to get the frosting for the tips of the sled," Dash told her friends. "If we are going to pull the sled, we'll need to make sure the blades are smooth enough to glide over the ground." Her wings fluttered and she shot up in the air. "This sled is going to be *so mint*!"

Raina knew her friends would come together to make this happen. "I'll stay here and keep Lyra comfortable," she said. "Dash, do you think we'll be able to get Lyra to the castle before Sun Dip?"

"Yes," she said, "I do." Then she smiled. "I'm not sure we'll win any races, but we can get Lyra there before dark."

The fairies all flew off to get their supplies. Before the sun reached the very top of the mountains, the fairies were back at Fruit Chew Meadow.

True to Dash's promise, she built a sled with all the materials her friends had gathered. Soon they had a sled large enough for a unicorn in the meadow.

Melli and Berry held up the licorice ropes.

"We braided them to make them stronger," Melli said.

"Sweet and strong," Dash said. "I should get you all to work on my next sled with me." She attached the frosted licorice blades to the sled and then stood back to admire the finished product. "Not bad," she said, checking over the sled. "I think we're about done."

Raina was feeding Lyra tiny bits of rainbow gummy chews when she heard Dash's news. Lyra's horn was still dull and the unicorn had not spoken or sung a word. Raina tried not to show her concern, but she was very worried.

"The sled is finished," Dash said.

The five fairies surrounded Lyra. They each took a piece of the blanket she was lying on and gently lifted the unicorn to the sled. Dash had done a great job of measuring the seat. The sled was perfect for Lyra.

"Sour sugars," Raina gasped. She pointed to Lyra's horn. Instead of being dull, the horn was now black. "We have to get her to Candy Castle right away!"

CHAPTER

7

A Sweet Ride

"Grab hold!" Raina instructed as she tossed the licorice ropes out to her friends.

The fairies worked together to pull the large sled through Fruit Chew Meadow. Each of them held on tight to the braided red licorice ropes and pulled with all her might. As they passed Red Licorice Lake, no one spoke a word. Each fairy was concentrating on pulling the sled—and getting the sick unicorn to the castle.

"Not much farther," Raina called over her shoulder. Glancing back at Lyra, she saw that the unicorn was resting comfortably on the sled. Only her horn made her seem different. Raina didn't have to look *that* fact up in the Fairy Code Book. A dull black horn was not a sign of a healthy unicorn.

"Dash, this sled is smooth as caramel," Melli said. "I can't believe we are pulling Lyra all the way to the castle."

"This is one smooth, sweet ride," Berry added.

Up ahead Raina saw the tall sugar cube walls of Candy Castle come into view. Never had Raina been so happy to see the pink-and-white sugarcoated castle! If anyone could save the unicorn, it was Princess Lolli.

As the fairies neared the front gate the castle guards came out to greet them. Quickly the guards took over and pulled Lyra through the gates into the Royal Gardens. They had been expecting the sick unicorn, and they were ready for her.

Princess Lolli came out to the garden. "I knew you would get Lyra here," she said to the fairies. She took a step back to admire the sled they had built. "This is extraordinary!"

"We all worked together," Raina spoke up. She turned to smile at Dash. "But this was Dash's design."

Dash blushed. "Sure as sugar, it helped to

have a Caramel, Gummy, Fruit, and Chocolate Fairy around," she said.

The fairy princess laughed. "Well done," she said. "And we are all so grateful." She waved her hand toward the large front door. "Come, let's get Lyra inside. We have a special vanilla bath waiting for her."

"Will she be all right?" Raina asked. She watched as the sled was pulled inside the castle. "Her horn has turned black," she said in a hushed voice.

Princess Lolli put her arm around Raina. "Yes, I saw that," she said gently. "I was worried that might happen. But now that Lyra is here, we'll be able to help her. The vanilla bath will get rid of any trace of salt." She smiled at Raina. "Lyra is going to be fine. Your getting her here quickly saved her."

Raina lowered her head. If only she had gotten to Fruit Chew Meadow earlier! She should have listened to Dash. If she had, they would have found Lyra sooner. And maybe the unicorn would not be this ill.

"Raina, this isn't your fault," Berry whispered in her ear. She came up beside her friend when she saw the worried look on Raina's face. "The important thing is that we got Lyra here to the castle. Now she can get help."

Hearing Berry say this to her made Raina feel worse. She should not have taken that nap after lunch. She and Dash could have been in the meadow to stop Mogu.

Dash flew over to Raina and gently pulled her away from the others. "Mogu stirred up trouble long before we got to Fruit Chew Meadow," she told her. "Berry is right. At least now Lyra is safe here at the castle."

"But I . . . ," Raina started to say. Tears gathered in her eyes.

Holding up her hand, Dash cut Raina off. "No one is more considerate of the animals in Sugar Valley than you," she said firmly. "Please don't be upset. If we're going to get Fruit Chew Meadow back to normal, we have to get Mogu out of there tonight. We can do it."

"Thank you, Dash," Raina said. She wiped away her tears and took a deep breath. "I guess

the important thing now is to find a way to keep that salty troll out of the meadow."

"And those Chuchies," Dash grumbled.

"How about we fix the fence first?" Melli called over to her friends. "We have leftover caramel from the sled already at the meadow. We can use that to patch up the hole."

"If this is Mogu's work," Raina said, "a fence won't keep him out. Fences don't keep trolls out." She sat down under a gummy tree in the Royal Gardens. "We need to find a way to trick Mogu—or at least teach him a lesson."

"I had a feeling she was going to say that," Dash said, smiling. She sat down next to Raina.

"He can't keep bringing salt into the meadow," Melli said. "You'd think that he'd notice the damage he's done to the flowers and Lyra."

"Mogu only cares about himself," Cocoa told her friends.

"Too bad we don't know another unicorn with a rainbow horn," joked Berry. "That would make Mogu jump."

Raina flew straight up in the air. Her wings were moving as fast as the thoughts in her head. "I know how we can trick that salty troll!" Raina shouted. "First I need to get something from Gummy Forest. I'll meet you all back at Fruit Chew Meadow at the end of Sun Dip."

Before her friends could ask any questions, Raina raced off to Gummy Forest. She hoped with all her heart that her plan to trick Mogu would work. She never wanted to see Lyra looking so sick again. And she had a few hours left to save Berry's birthday—and Valentine's Day!

CHAPTER
8

A Gummy Good Idea

Raina sped through Gummy Forest. The sun was heading quickly toward the top of the Frosted Mountains. She didn't have much time! Raina worked quickly and gathered all she needed for her plan. She had to get back to Fruit Chew Meadow before dark.

This has to trick Mogu, she thought. If she could

get Mogu and the Chuchies out of the meadow, the flowers would bounce back by morning and the meadow would be safe for Lyra. The fairies could celebrate Lyra's return—and Berry's birthday. This was a delicious plan!

The gummy cubs and bunnies watched Raina work. They were curious about what the Gummy Fairy was doing and crowded around her.

"Sweet sugar cubes!" Raina exclaimed. She looked over at the group of gummy animals. "What do you think?" A smile spread across her face as she held up her work.

The animals were not sure what Raina was creating, but they sensed it was exactly what she had set out to make.

"Oh, I hope this works," Raina said to the animals. She reached over to pet a blue gummy

bear on the head. "Be good, Blue Belle," she said. "Look after the others for me. I will be back soon."

When Raina arrived at Fruit Chew Meadow, the sky was a deep lavender with spots of pink swirls. Normally, Raina loved Sun Dip. She enjoyed talking to her friends, telling stories, and sampling the candy crops of the day. Only today Sun Dip was not about having fun. Today Sun Dip was about tricking a troll!

"Are you ready to teach Mogu a lesson?" Raina asked as she touched down next to her friends. They were all waiting near the berry cherry tree.

"Sure as sugar!" Berry replied.

"We mended the fence with hot caramel," Melli said. "Mogu will have a harder time getting into the meadow now."

Raina took her gummy creation out of her

bag. She held up the rainbow gummy unicorn horn proudly. "This should keep Mogu and the Chuchies out for a long, long time," she said.

Melli gasped. "Where'd you get that?"

"Is . . . is . . . is that Lyra's horn?" Dash asked. Her mouth hung open and her eyes were wide with disbelief.

"No, silly," Raina said. "It's a gummy cone from a pine gummy tree," she told her friends. She smiled slyly. "And then I added a little more gummy candy."

"Lickin' lollipops, Raina!" Berry exclaimed. "That looks just like Lyra's horn!"

Raina's wings fluttered. She blushed a little too. "I was hoping you'd say that," she admitted. "The real test is if Mogu and the Chuchies think this is really Lyra's horn."

"What are you planning?" Cocoa asked.

Leaning in toward her friends, Raina spoke softly. "I was thinking if we hid in the bushes and poked this horn out, Mogu would get spooked that Lyra is back." She raised her eyebrows. "What do you think?"

"Holy peppermint!" Dash burst out. "You are *so mint*, Raina."

Her friends all nodded in agreement.

"It's a gummy good idea!" Cocoa blurted out.

Raina was glad her friends thought her idea would work. She hoped the horn would fool Mogu and the Chuchies.

The five fairies crept along the hedges lining the edge of the meadow. They didn't have to wait long. Soon they saw Mogu and the Chuchies approaching the gate. As they got closer Raina felt her stomach flip-flop. Seeing Mogu in his clunky boots caked with salt made her so mad.

"Just look at him," Berry snarled. "He doesn't even care that the salt on his boots made Lyra sick."

Dash popped up in between Raina and Berry. "Maybe he didn't know?" she asked.

Raina watched the grumpy, greedy troll. His big belly hung over his pants, and his white hair stuck up in a ring around his huge head. "He doesn't seem very concerned about anyone but himself—and his tummy."

"Well, look at this!" Mogu grumbled. He stopped in front of the mended fence. "Seems someone fixed the fence." He stuck his chocolate-stained fingers into the caramel patch, which had not dried yet.

"Yummmm," he said, licking his finger. "Fresh caramel is *sooooooo* good."

Melli's face turned a bright cherry red. She bit her lip so she would keep quiet.

Raina hunched down low and rustled the leaves in the bushes. Now was the time to get this show started! She slipped the gummy horn onto a stick.

"Meeeeeeeeeeee, meeeeee!" the Chuchies shouted, jumping up and down on their short, skinny legs. Their furry, round yellow bodies shook as they jumped.

"Shhhh," snapped Mogu. He held his hand up to quiet the Chuchies. Looking around, he narrowed his eyes. "What was that?" he asked.

"Meeeeeeeee, meeeeeee?" the Chuchies asked.

Raina rustled the bush branches again.

"Couldn't be," Mogu muttered. He pushed down on the caramel fence where the caramel was still soft, and he broke through.

Holding tight, Raina swayed the rainbow gummy pinecone around. Then she stuck the horn through the bush.

"Salty sticks!" Mogu exclaimed. "How can that be?" He rubbed his eyes. The light was fading fast. "She's back?"

Raina looked over at Berry. Now was her time to sing! Berry nodded and smiled at Raina.

"Gentle breeze and sweet light, flavors of the rainbow grow bright . . . ," Berry sang out.

Raina was impressed by how similar Berry sounded to Lyra. As she sang Raina moved the horn just as if Lyra was there. When Berry finished the song, Dash popped her head up over the bush.

"They're leaving!" Dash cried.

All the fairies peered over the bush. Raina couldn't believe her eyes. Mogu and the Chuchies were running away!

9

Three Delicious Reasons

Are they really gone?" Raina asked. She squinted her eyes to see in the early evening dim light.

"Yes!" Dash cheered. "The gummy pinecone trick worked!"

"Raina, that was *choc-o-rific*!" Cocoa blurted out. "You fooled Mogu."

Melli fluttered her wings and lifted off the ground. "And I don't think he'll be coming back anytime soon," she added. "I didn't think that Mogu could move that fast."

"Oh, we have to let Lyra know," Berry said. "I can't wait to see the look on her face." She turned to Raina. "Thank you. On behalf of all the Fruit Fairies—and all Candy Fairies—thank you!"

"Do you want us to go with you?" Melli asked.

Berry shook her head. "No, I'll go," she told her friends. "I feel bad that I wasn't here earlier to help Lyra. I was at Lollipop Landing this morning, and I wish I had been here." She lowered her head and fingered her fruit-chew bracelet. "If I'd been here, I would have been able to stop Mogu, and Lyra wouldn't be so sick."

At that moment Raina realized that she wasn't the only one feeling responsible for Lyra's misfortune. When something so sour happened, everyone felt bad.

"You know," Raina said to her friend, "we all feel responsible. I was thinking that if I had come earlier to the meadow, I could have stopped Mogu too."

Berry looked up at Raina.

"Me too," Dash said.

"We were thinking the same thing," Melli said, pointing at herself and Cocoa.

"I guess the important thing is that we did get here," Raina told them. "Lyra is getting help and Mogu is gone."

A smile appeared on Berry's face. "You're right," she said. "Thank you." She sniffed a little.

"I'll see you tomorrow. Red Licorice Lake for Sun Dip?"

"It's a plan," Raina said, giving her friend a hug.

As Berry headed off to Candy Castle, Raina looked around at Dash, Cocoa, and Melli.

"I think Berry forgot that tomorrow is her birthday!" she said. "What do you think of having a surprise party in Fruit Chew Meadow?" Raina saw her friends grinning. "It will be a triply sweet celebration—a homecoming for Lyra, a birthday party for Berry, and a Valentine's Day surprise for all Candy Fairies."

"Berry will love the idea," Cocoa said.

"She deserves a supersweet surprise for her birthday," Melli added.

A sugar fly landed on Raina's shoulder. The envelope was from Princess Lolli.

Princess Lolli
Candy Castle
Sugar Valley
Candy Kingdom

Lyra is doing well.
She enjoyed her
vanilla bath, and her
horn is back to normal.
She is going to be fine.
Many thanks to you and
your friends,
Princess Lolli.

"This must be news about Lyra," Raina said, opening up the note. "Dash, could you hold up a mint stick so I can read this? I hope this is good news."

Dash held up a bright mint stick as the fairies huddled around Raina. They were anxious to hear the royal news.

"Lyra is doing well," Raina read. "She enjoyed

her vanilla bath, and her horn is back to normal. She is going to be fine. Many thanks to you and your friends, Princess Lolli."

"So mint!" Dash exclaimed. "Now we definitely need to plan a celebration."

Raina took out a notebook from her bag. "We don't have much time to pull this party together. So we'll have to be fast." She started making a list. "First we need to try to keep this a secret. Part of the fun will be surprising Berry."

"And Lyra," Cocoa added.

Tapping her pen on her notebook, Raina tried to think of all the ingredients for a good party. "First, we need to send out invites with the sugar flies. We'll have to make sure to write Top Secret so no one tells Berry about the party."

Melli peered over Raina's shoulder to look at her list. "How are we ever going to pull this party together by Sun Dip tomorrow?"

"Wait, there's Fruli," Dash said, pointing to the far end of the meadow. "Maybe she can help out."

Fruli spotted the fairies under Dash's mint glow and came over to them. "Is Lyra feeling better?" she asked when she saw the fairies. "I heard from a sugar fly that you brought her to Candy Castle on a sled."

"Yes," Raina said. "She's feeling much better."

"And we just tricked Mogu, so he won't be tracking in salt near the meadow again," Dash told her. "At least, not for a long time."

Fruli smiled. "Oh, I am glad to hear that," she

said. She shuddered. "I've never met Mogu—and I don't want to!"

Raina shrugged. "Oh, he's not that bad," she said. "Just a little salty."

Stepping forward, Raina moved closer to Fruli. "Tomorrow is Berry's birthday," she told her. "We'd like to surprise Berry with a party and also welcome Lyra home. We don't have much time, and we could really use your help."

"How delicious! I would love to help!" Fruli exclaimed. "I didn't know Berry's birthday was on Valentine's Day. I'll have to make her a special heart valentine."

"How about helping with the decorations for the meadow?" Raina asked.

Fruli clapped her hands. "I could do that!" she said. "My aunt just gave me this fabulous

blueberry and cherry material from Meringue Island. We could use it as a tablecloth or something and then get some rainbow lollipops to stick around."

Raina knew she had just asked the right fairy for the job. With Fruli's great design taste, she was sure Fruit Chew Meadow would look *sugar-tacular* by tomorrow's Sun Dip.

"Sure as sugar, this meadow is going to look supersweet," Raina said. "It will be a sugarcoated celebration." She smiled at her friends. "Now we just have to keep the secret from Berry!"

CHAPTER
10

A Sugarcoated Day

Raina was up the next morning bright and early. She had so much to do! Not only did she have to feed the animals in Gummy Forest, she had a party to plan!

She'd have to do all her work in the forest quickly and then head to Fruit Chew Meadow. Knowing that she wouldn't have time to fly back home, Raina decided to take her party clothes with her now. Racing around her room, Raina folded her clothes neatly into her backpack. Half of Sugar Valley was coming to Berry and Lyra's surprise party that evening. If everything was going to be finished by Sun Dip, she had to hurry.

Luckily, the gummy animals were well-behaved, and feeding time went well. Thankful that the animals were calm and listening to instructions, Raina gave each one a little extra flavoring. "After all," she told them, "today is a day to celebrate!"

As Raina was cleaning out the gummy bears' feeding log, Melli suddenly appeared before her. The Caramel Fairy's face was bright red, and even when she landed her wings didn't stop fluttering.

"Raina!" Melli gasped. "Oh, I'm so glad I found you here."

Raina dropped the log in the water. "Is Lyra all right?" Raina asked. "What's wrong? Did you hear something?" She eyed her friend's nervous expression.

Melli put her hand up and tried desperately to catch her breath. "Everything is fine," she said. "In fact, everything is more than fine." She smiled. "I'm just bursting to tell you the sweet news!"

"What?" Raina asked. She couldn't imagine what news Melli had for her.

"Guess who is coming to the party tonight?" Melli finally managed to say.

The guest list for the party had gotten so long that Raina had lost count of all the fairies invited. She shook her head. "I don't know," she said, playing along with Melli. "Who?"

"The Sugar Pops!" Melli shouted. Once she said the musical group's name, her wings started flapping again and she soared up to the sky. "Berry is going to flip!"

All the Candy Fairies loved the three brothers who made up the Sugar Pops. Chip, Char, and Carob were three of the most delicious singers. Their music was always at the top of the charts in Sugar Valley.

"That *is* sweet news!" Raina exclaimed. "How do you know? Are you sure?"

The Caramel Fairy nodded quickly. "I was at Candy Castle early this morning to make a delivery, and I saw Princess Lolli," Melli explained. "She told me that Lyra is going home later today and that she'd heard all about the plans for the surprise party." Melli grabbed Raina's hands and started to jump up and down. "And then she told me that Dash had sent a sugar fly to Carob Pop! She let him know about Lyra's being sick, Berry's birthday, and the Valentine's Day celebration. Carob sent her back a sugar fly! Can you believe it?"

Raina shook her head. She was in sugar shock!

"He said he wanted to come sing with Lyra tonight at Sun Dip to help the flowers," Melli continued. She stopped jumping and sank down onto the ground. "Isn't that just the sweetest thing ever?" she swooned.

"Sure as sugar," Raina said.

Melli helped Raina pick up the feeding log and carry it over to the edge of the water. Finally

Melli's wings slowed down, and she was able to breathe normally.

"Having the Sugar Pops sing at the party tonight will sweeten the whole night," Raina said. She grinned at Melli. "Dash found the perfect surprise for Berry."

"And everyone in Sugar Valley!" Melli added.

Raina stuck her hand out and pulled Melli up. "Now we really have to make sure the meadow is looking good," she said. "We're going to have a huge party!"

"I know!" Melli exclaimed. "That's why I had to come here and tell you!"

"And you're sure Berry doesn't know?" Raina asked.

Melli shook her head. "All the sugar flies and fairies know the party is a surprise." Melli grinned. "I have to make sure I don't see Berry today. I don't think I can keep the secret."

Raina rubbed her wet hands on her dress. "I know how you feel," she said. "I'm going to have to avoid Berry all day too! Fruli is going to be with her most of the day and promised to keep her away from the meadow."

"Yes, I heard," Melli said. "And they will escort Lyra back at Sun Dip, right?"

"That's the plan," Raina said. She held up her crossed fingers. "I hope all goes well. I want this to be an extra-special surprise for them both!"

Melli gave Raina a hug. She took off, and called over her shoulder, "I'll see you at Sun Dip!"

Raina stood for a moment, smiling. Their plans were coming together: Lyra was healthy, Berry was going to have a birthday surprise, and now the Sugar Pops were going to sing! This was turning out to be a sugarcoated Valentine's Day.

For Raina, the day was spent making candy for the party and organizing the decorations. She had a quick visit with Lyra at the castle and was happy to see her feeling well.

Back at the meadow, plans for the party were going perfectly. Fruli had dropped off the gorgeous Meringue Island material, and Raina, Cocoa, and Dash hung it as a curtain on the stage.

"For once I'm glad that Berry is always late," Dash said as she hung mint lights around the stage. "I hope we finish in time!"

"Everything looks great," Raina said happily as she took in the scene.

The meadow looked beautiful with the festive decorations, and the flowers were all standing up straight.

"We actually pulled this together!" Dash exclaimed.

"Here they come!" Cocoa shouted. "Places, everyone!"

The fairies all gathered around the stage while the Sugar Pops played. Raina could see the surprised expressions on Berry's and Lyra's faces as they got closer. When the two of them landed on the stage, everyone applauded.

Berry just gazed around the meadow with her mouth open.

"I don't think I've ever seen Berry speechless!" Raina said, giving her friend a tight squeeze. "Happy birthday!"

"I can't think of a sweeter surprise for my birthday *and* Valentine's Day," Berry said. "Thank you all so much." She turned to Raina, Dash, Melli, and Cocoa. "You did all this?"

"Yes," Raina said. "We all helped. Especially Fruli."

Raina handed Berry a present. She was so excited to give Berry her birthday gift. When Raina had visited Lyra earlier that day at Candy Castle, Lyra had told her about the flower she had grown especially for Berry.

"Oh, Raina!" Berry cried. "This is scrumptious!" She put the headband on her head. "I love the fruit-chew flower and all the sparkly gummies."

"I'm glad you like it," Raina said. "Happy birthday, Berry." She went over to Lyra and

stroked her long nose. "And welcome home, Lyra."

Lyra nuzzled Raina's hand. "Thank you," she sang out.

The fairies all exchanged cards and other treats. The whole kingdom was there to celebrate the festive day.

"This turned out to be the sweetest Valentine's Day surprise," Berry said to her friends. "Lyra is healthy, the meadow looks great, and the Sugar Pops are here!"

Raina looked over at Dash and smiled. "Sure as sugar!" she exclaimed happily.

The Sugar Pops played well past when the sun slid behind the Frosted Mountains. Everyone was having a deliciously sweet time.

"This was the best Valentine's Day ever!"

Berry exclaimed at the end of the night.

"And I got some great gifts too," Dash said, grinning.

"Who doesn't love Valentine's Day?" Cocoa added.

Melli and Raina laughed.

"We all got some sweet surprises," Raina said. "But the sweetest part is that we helped Lyra."

"Look at Lyra now," Dash said, smiling.

Lyra was in the meadow, away from the crowds. She was softly singing her special lullaby to the flowers.

"Do you think she liked the party?" Raina asked.

"Yes," Berry said, hugging Raina. "And she loves being back safe and sound, surrounded by all these friends."

Raina smiled. This *was* a grand birthday and Valentine's Day event. There was no better way to celebrate Berry's birthday and Lyra's homecoming. They had tricked Mogu once again, and the Sugar Pops were playing. The sounds coming from the meadow were joyous and sweet. It was a perfect Candy Fairy celebration full of love and friendship!

Bubble Gum Rescue

Early in the morning, Melli the Caramel Fairy flew to the top of Caramel Hills. She was checking on the caramel chocolate rolls she had made with her Chocolate Fairy friend Cocoa. Melli smiled at their newest creation drying in the cool shade of a caramel tree. Yesterday the two fairies had worked hard rolling small logs of caramel and then dipping them in chocolate. The final touch was a drizzle of butterscotch on top. Melli couldn't wait to taste one!

A caramel turtle jutted his head out of his shell and smelled the fresh candy. Melli laughed. "You were hiding over by that log," she said to the turtle. She kneeled down next to him. "Did you think you'd snatch a candy without my noticing?"

The turtle quickly slipped his head back into his shell. Still as a rock, he waited to see what the Caramel Fairy would do.

Melli placed one of the candies in front of him. "Of course you may have one," she said sweetly. "There's enough to share."

The turtle stuck his head out again and gobbled it up.

"Do you like the candy?" Melli asked.

The turtle nodded, and Melli smiled. "Cocoa and I are going to bring these to Sun Dip this evening," she said.

Sun Dip was the time at the end of the day when the sun set behind the Frosted Mountains and the Candy Fairies relaxed. Melli loved visiting with her friends and catching up on everyone's activities. And today she and Cocoa would bring their new candy. She hoped her friends would enjoy the sweet treat.

Just as Melli was putting the candies in her basket, she heard a squeal. It sounded like an animal in trouble. She put the basket down and walked toward the sound.

"Hot caramel!" Melli cried as she peered around one of the caramel trees.

Lying on the ground was a small caramella bird. He was trying to flap his wings to fly, but they were barely moving. Melli leaned in closer and noticed that the bird's feathers were wet and stuck together.

Melli reached out to the bird. "You poor thing," she whispered. She tried to calm the little one by talking to him. Caramella birds lived in the valley of Caramel Hills and had bright yellow wing feathers. They lived off the seeds of the caramel trees and filled the hills with their soft chirps.

"Where have you been playing?" Melli asked sweetly. She carefully picked up the bird and gently stroked his head. Immediately she realized that his feathers were covered in thick butterscotch. "How did you get coated in this syrup?" she asked. "No wonder you can't move or fly."

The bird chirped loudly. It was shaking in her hands.

"Butterscotch is not the best thing for feathers," Melli said, smiling at the tiny caramella. "Don't worry, sweetie," she added softly. "Let's give you a good bath and get this mess off your wings. I know all about sticky caramel." She patted the bird's head gently. "I will get you cleaned up in no time. Let's go to the water well and rinse you off."

Melli held on to the bird and flew to the edge of Caramel Hills. The tiny creature seemed to relax in Melli's hands, but his heart was still pounding. At the well Melli began to wash the butterscotch off the bird's wings. She knew she'd have to spend some time scrubbing. She had gotten caramel on her clothes before, and it often took a while to get all the goo off.

After a few rinses Melli began to see his brightly colored feathers.

"There, that does it," she said, feeling satisfied. She stood back and looked at the little bird. "You do have gorgeous yellow wings!"

The bird shook the water off his wings. He was happy to be able to move them freely. He bowed his head to Melli, thanking her for helping him.

"You should be able to fly now," Melli said. "Be careful, and stay away from the sticky stuff!"

"Hi, Melli!" Cocoa appeared next to her. "What are you doing here?"

"Cocoa," Melli gasped. "You scared me!

I didn't see you there." She pointed to the caramella bird. "Look who I found. He was covered in butterscotch, and his wings were stuck together. I just gave him a bath with the fresh well water."

Cocoa's wings fluttered. "Oh, bittersweet chocolate," she said sadly. "This is worse than I thought."

"What are you talking about?" Melli asked. "He's all clean now. He'll be able to fly."

"It's not only this bird I am worried about," Cocoa said. "I heard from a sugar fly that there was a butterscotch syrup spill on the eastern side of Butterscotch Volcano. That must be where this one got syrup on his wings. *All* the caramella birds are in danger!"

"Oh no," Melli said. "So many caramella birds

live over there. What else did the sugar fly tell you?"

"That was all," Cocoa replied.

Sugar flies passed information around Sugar Valley. If a fairy wanted to get the word out about something important, the sugar flies were the ones to spread the news. "Let's go now," Melli said urgently. "If Butterscotch Volcano erupts, there'll be a large spill in the hills." She looked down at the bird. "Is that what happened to you? Will you take us to where you got butterscotch on your wings?"

The bird took flight, and Melli and Cocoa trailed after him. His yellow feathers gleamed in the sunlight. Melli beat her wings faster. She was very concerned about what kind of sticky mess they were going to find.

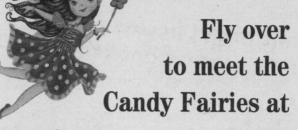